About the Author

Pete Cross is a new author with a penchant for adventure, driven by his love for the sporty outdoor life and his family's desire to travel.

Living in Leicester, England with his wife and two sons and with a successful career as a Director in the National Health Service and an academic Doctorate to his name, his aspiration to inspire others to explore and seek out different challenges is reflected in his writing.

For Jack and Charlie – the sky is not your limit, it is only the limit of your sight. Go explore!

Pete Cross

THE ROCKWALL BROTHERS

AUSTIN MACAULEY PUBLISHERS™
LONDON · CAMBRIDGE · NEW YORK · SHARJAH

Copyright © Pete Cross (2017)

The right of Pete Cross to be identified as author of this work has been asserted by him in accordance with section 77 and 78 of the Copyright, Designs and Patents Act 1988.

All rights reserved. No part of this publication may be reproduced, stored in a retrieval system, or transmitted in any form or by any means, electronic, mechanical, photocopying, recording, or otherwise, without the prior permission of the publishers.

Any person who commits any unauthorised act in relation to this publication may be liable to criminal prosecution and civil claims for damages.

A CIP catalogue record for this title is available from the British Library.

ISBN 9781788234351 (Paperback)
ISBN 9781788234368 (Hardback)
ISBN 9781788234375 (E-Book)
www.austinmacauley.com

First Published (2017)
Austin Macauley Publishers Ltd.
25 Canada Square
Canary Wharf
London
E14 5LQ

Chapter 1
Pier 57, Uptown, New York City

Twenty-third of October 2017
All he could hear was the sound of his own breath. He knew he needed to calm down and focus on the surrounding environment but his breath was like a siren in his ears. "Slow down, think, slow down, think," he kept on repeating it over and over as he ducked behind some old stacked wooden crates that barely provided him with cover. The old unused pier, Pier Fifty-seven, had been his temporary camp for the last few hours. Then he heard the echo of the following footsteps; he hadn't shrugged them off, they had tracked him to his Uptown New York hideout. His life slowed down in that moment. Where was his brother? He always looked out for him, his older brother always did that, no matter how much he tried to play the annoying little brother, Jack was always there when he needed him. Charlie remembered when he had stepped in when Samuel from year six tried to snatch his best football trading card, Jack was only year five but big for his age and popular; popular was as good a survival attribute at school as being able to stand up for yourself in a fight, no-one picked on the popular ones unless you were the most unpopular one. Sam was, no-one liked him

and he liked no-one. Charlie was popular but only in year three and was one of the smaller ones for his age. After Jack stood towering over Sam, with his faithful gang in back-up, Sam soon backed down and it taught Charlie a lesson. Jack had never had a fight with anyone but just showing the intent was enough to make Sam think twice. This was not the playground though, this was for real. The big-time villains in pursuit of the heroes sounded familiar from the stories that he read but this was no fictional story, he couldn't just put the book down, turn out the light and go to sleep.

The footsteps kept coming nearer and nearer, near enough to be able to smell the days of musty grime on his pursuer, near enough to see his shadow. The shadow had trailed them for the last twenty-four hours, Charlie was feeling the tiredness that only came from having to be alert for that length of time. He slipped back into 'life in slow motion' mode. Where was Jack? How could he leave his eight-year-old brother in this mess? How had a family trip to London ended up with him here on his own? He thought back to what his mum always said to him—no, not about 'loving him all the bags of sugar in the world,' that just embarrassed him. (Well, he secretly liked it but wouldn't openly admit it.) His mum always said that his family, Mum, Dad, Jack and Charlie, were like a rock wall. The wall was at its strongest with all of the rocks in place; if you took any one of the rocks away, then the whole wall was in danger of collapsing. Was that rock wall about to crumble?

Charlie's inner thoughts were interrupted by an almighty explosion, BOOM! He almost laughed out loud. That was Jack's entrance, he knew he would come. The Shadow's footsteps swiftly changed direction and disappeared away from the furore of the blast. Jack ghosted in through a concealment of smoke and noise, lifted him up with a reassuring wink and placed a brotherly arm around his shoulder. They had a peek at the package, still in one piece, they were still in one piece, their adventure showed no sign of letting up!

Chapter 2
Home, Leicester, England

Fourteenth of October 2017
The boys had been building up to this point for the last two weeks, ever since Mum and Dad had told them that they were going to London for half term, 'The Smoke'. The Shard, the London Eye, Buckingham Palace, *HMS Belfast* and lots of staying up late. School was closed for the October half term so all that was left was to pack their rucksacks with books, toys and football trading cards for the time spent in the Premier Lodge and wait for the morning.

Jack and Charlie Cross, two normal brothers from a normal family who lived on a normal housing estate in a normal village on the outskirts of Leicester. In fact, they lived a very down-to-earth normal life. They even behaved like normal brothers, not wanting to admit what good friends they were, not wanting to agree on the same things to play, not wanting to show how proud they were of each other. And if you met them, then you wouldn't even think they were brothers. Jack was ten years old, tall and slim (he was a full head above his class-mates), blonde hair, hazel-green eyes and a driven personality and will to succeed that sometimes sent his usual placid temperament over the edge or what Mum and Dad called 'his red mist'. He was what you would call 'text book' clever, well-read (and he read loads of books), intelligent and top of the class at most subjects. Charlie was also clever. He had large bright blue eyes, dark hair and his sparkly grin helped him get out of trouble from the mischief that seemed to follow him around. He was small for his year but gained attention for his looks, but one should never mention 'Charlie' and 'cute' in the same sentence, he hated being called that. Mum and Dad could see the idolisation that he held for his older brother but he became embarrassed if they ever pointed it out, too cool to show his love.

So what did they have in common? Football, sport, books, more football and a passion for adventure and experiencing something new. That was it, nothing more, nothing less. Their time together was mainly spent in the garden re-enacting the latest Jimmy Farvey goal, their favourite City player, or honing their football skills so that when Carl Spearhead, the City manager, came calling for them to pull on the City shirt then they would be ready, no more watching their heroes on a Saturday afternoon from the stand, they dreamed of being part of it.

However, despite their perceived normality, it was the break from the normal things that always got them excited, the holidays, the new places to see, living out of a suitcase and the anticipation in the build-up to these experiences. Jack and Charlie appreciated that Mum and Dad worked really hard to give them these opportunities to travel and Dad spent a lot of time working away, ironically, in London. Doing what, they didn't know. They knew he wore smart suits, spent a lot of time on his phone when he was at home and he said he was an accountant but they didn't really know what one of those did. Still, undaunted by the unknown, an accountant was on Charlie's list of jobs to do when he became a grown-up, along with professional footballer and spaceman.

When he was at home, Dad spent his time in the garden with the boys, also trying to hone his football skills and, at thirty-eight, still awaiting that call from Carl Spearhead. He always asked Mum in front of the boys who was the better footballer that she had seen play live, him or Leo Messi? And of course, Mum always had to answer that Dad was the best (as she had never seen Messi play in the flesh). The boys always mocked Dad's jokes and faked not being amused but, even when he was claiming to have had deadly lasers fitted to his eyes after having laser eye surgery, they loved the banter and the messing around and wouldn't want to change it for the world.

Despite Dad's continued denial, Jack and Charlie had crowned Mum as the boss of the family. Mum dedicated her life to kids, not just her own but she also held a part-time job working in the village nursery. She spent more time with the boys and you could tell that her own values and standards were being reflected in her own children. Please and thank yous were non-negotiable and you would know about it if you forgot your manners. Treat people how you expect to be treated yourself, work hard and smile after the job is done and don't trust anyone until they have earned that trust. (She always drilled in to Jack and Charlie the mantra, 'Never let anyone ride your bike,' – meaning, don't trust others with things that are precious to you.) On the surface, Mum was straight talking and strong-willed, but underneath that feisty exterior was the lynchpin of the family; caring, understanding and proud of her boys, even Dad!

The Crosses were a normal but strong unit of a family. Mum referred to them as the rock wall, and they were about to hit the lights of London. Jack and Charlie went to sleep that night with their usual innocence of expectation, unaware of the twists and turns about to announce themselves.

Chapter 3
Welcome to London

"Are we nearly there yet?" piped up Charlie. "My legs are aching!"

A day up the Shard, playing footie in Green Park, scoffing posh chocolate and fighting off the German U-boats on *HMS Belfast* had taken its toll on his energy levels.

"Are we nearly where?" asked Dad.

"The hotel, I'm reeeeeally tired!" pronounced Charlie.

"Too tired for a surprise then?" teased Dad.

"What? Where? Why?" Charlie always asked rapid-fire questions when he was excited.

"Well, I'll only tell you if you apologise."

"For what?" retorted Charlie.

"You know," replied Dad, and Charlie did.

Jack and Charlie had spent the whole of the trip up the Shard torturing Dad for his fear of heights, pretending to hang off the edge and fall, pointing out the parachutist ready to jump from the highest point so Dad had to look directly up, sending him dizzy then breaking out in fits of laughter when he realised there was no-one there. The boys were in 'high five' heaven, cruel but funny, but now it was time for Dad to get his own back.

"Actually, thinking about it now, I couldn't possibly stretch to another surprise."

"Daaaaad!" Jack and Charlie chorused.

"Say it," Dad playfully demanded. "Say it out loud."

"We're sorry," Jack mumbled.

"Sorry, can't hear you."

"We're sorry," Jack repeated, a little louder.

"No, not good enough. Charlie, you're right, let's go back to the hotel," Dad smiled.

"Stop being such a tease," said Mum.

"Okay, we can have the surprise, if you do one thing," Dad continued. Jack and Charlie looked hopeful.

"You strut your best dance moves right here in the street and I'll let you have the surprise."

They were standing in the middle of Westminster Bridge, ready to return to their County Hall Hotel on the South Bank, a packed street with people scurrying along like ants, bumping into each other but never acknowledging each other. London was like that, atmospheric but impersonal. Charlie immediately broke out in to his best dance moves that he'd practised with his mates at the last school disco, much to the delight of Mum who was whooping and almost joining in with his moves. Passers-by shared in the family moment with either a scowl of disgust that these tourists should dare to delay their own journey from the office or with wry smiles of appreciation for the togetherness that they openly showed. Charlie finished his routine by toppling over into Dad, who just managed to stop him falling in front of an umbrella-wielding businessman, who looked highly unamused.

"Right, your turn, Jack," Dad cajoled.

"No, it's embarrassing," Jack refused.

"No surprise then, simple," Dad smirked. "I'll teach you to tease me."

Jack's mood instantly changed to a level of grumpiness that on the 'Jack Grumpy Scale' was only deemed as a mild mood swing but would probably have been moderate on normal scales. Jack's moods were legendary in the family, only rivalled by Mum herself but Mum always used the excuse that it was living with three boys that sent her to that point. Dad knew to play to Jack's competitive side when he saw the early signs of the mood swings. "Well, we'll just have to get off home then, if you can't handle it!" (Dad always referred to the hotel as home when they went away, not sure why but he always did it.) The intensity increased in Jack's eyes, his face flushed red, his body language suggested a meltdown and then— he broke into smile and pulled off his best dancing goal celebration. Mum whooped and clapped again.

"Right, to the toy shop," Dad declared.

According to Jack's new diver's watch, that his grandparents had bought him for his birthday the week before, it was 7.42 p.m. The big toy shops closed at eight p.m., too late. He felt the disappointment wash over him.

"We'll need to get a taxi," said Mum, as she held out her hand to flag a black cab down. Jack looked puzzled and Mum read the body language.

"We know a place that opens late. It's not big but you'll love it, almost magical."

Twenty minutes later, they pulled up to Portsmouth Street, Dad paid the driver and they all clambered out.

Chapter 4
The Toy Shop

"The Old Curiosity Shop." Dad dramatically pointed to a quirky building located on the corner of Portsmouth Street. It looked like it had come straight out of the 1600s with a wonky red-tiled roof, green painted window frames that probably hid the old rotting wood underneath and a leaning, bendy shape to the white rendered front walls.

"Olde Worlde. Wow, it's really old but well cared for, a bit like your dad!" Mum chuckled.

"What a rubbish toy shop, it's tiny," Jack moaned out loud, not sharing Mum's love of the architecture.

Charlie remained oblivious to the differing views being shared. "Will it sell *Star Wars* toys, Mum?" He made his way towards the front door of the shop.

"Uh-ah," Dad stopped him in his tracks. "Not that way, this way in," as he nodded towards an archway that led under the building.

The archway was dark and musty. A scraggy-looking cat roamed between their legs as they made their way along an unlit brick corridor. Both the cat and Charlie involuntarily jumped as he accidentally trod on its tail and it let out a short, sharp screech. It made Charlie scurry up to the front with Dad, almost knocking his big brother into the wall as he dashed past him. Jack attempted to shove him back but missed and stumbled some more, much to his annoyance. Dad almost looked like he knew where he was going as he turned into another well-hidden archway which framed a large, solid oak door with a big knocker that had a sign hanging underneath that read:

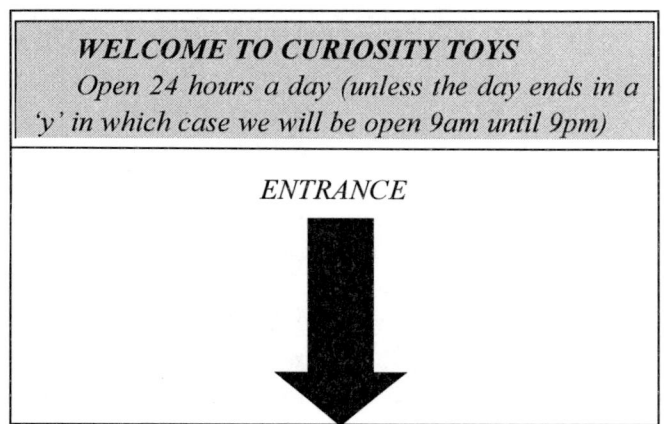

The arrow pointed directly to the cat flap and, as if to show how it should be done, the over-friendly cat jumped through the flap, leaving the squeaky-hinged door echoing in the enclosed corridor.

"Go on then, Charlie, you first, mate." Dad shifted his head towards the cat flap. Charlie looked up at Dad waiting for a smile but it didn't come. He eyed up the cat flap warily, then looked back up at Dad's now grinning face.

"Not funny," said Charlie as they, all but Charlie, broke into laughter that again echoed around the corridor as if it was twenty people, not three people, laughing.

Dad lifted Charlie up to bang the knocker but Jack sneaked in and beat him to it.

"Aaaargh," Charlie growled at Jack and aimed a soft but intended kick in his direction.

"Calm it down, you two," Mum intervened, "unless you want us to turn around and go back to the hotel?"

"Nooooo, sorry," they sang in unison.

The brief moment of tension was interrupted by a voice from behind the door, shouting, "I'll be there in a tick." Jack recognised the cockney accent as he had been picking it out as they had trekked around London and was planning to add it to his collection of accents that he would use in 'nonsense' conversations with his friends (apparently, that's what you do when you are ten years old). Scouse, Welsh and now cockney made up his collection, although when he did the impressions, they all started off well but ended up as a Scottish accent.

The Crosses waited for a few minutes in silence, just waiting, and waiting, and waiting, then there was some rustling behind the door and what seemed like about six different bolts being unlocked. A beady eye came to the gap in the door, spent a few seconds vetting the visitors, looking them up and down. You could feel the inquisitive nature of the character that was about to be revealed.

"You, password?" he poked a spindly finger through the gap and pointed at Jack.

"I don't know the password." Jack looked for reassurance from Mum.

"That's no good, guess it!" the beady eye demanded.

"I—I—I don't know." Jack paused for thought.

"Guess it, go on," the beady eye's voice was quite nasally and whiny.

"Erm—London?" Jack questioned. The door slammed shut. Jack looked apologetically at Mum, Dad and then Charlie, shrugged his shoulders and creased up his nose in a 'what was I supposed to say?' look. Then, the door suddenly swung open and the beady eye became a full beady man.

"How did you guess my password? You must be a mind-reader, young man!"

The man had the broadest smile across his face, which didn't match his vocal attributes. He was tall, skinny, in fact very tall, so tall he had to bend over to welcome them through the doorway. He had long, grey, wizard-like hair, a large thick nose which seemed out of proportion to the rest of his thin body and wide, boggly eyes that darted all over the place as he took in his new customers. Whilst quite strange in physical appearance, Jack didn't think that was the strangest part. He was wearing a white tuxedo with black bow tie, not the attire you would expect from a toy shop worker. He had an odd feeling come over him, an anxious, uncertain feeling that had now replaced his initial excitement. Mum's sixth sense kicked in and a reassuring arm came around his shoulder. It normally worked for him but this time the uncertain feeling remained.

"I'm Colin. Friends call me Curious Colin, after the name of the shop, you see." This seemed a well-rehearsed introduction but Charlie stifled a laugh; never had a name been so fitting. Jack would have normally joined in with Charlie's fun and egged him on but he was too busy trying to peer beyond Colin in to the shop behind him.

"Please come in, yes, do come in, out of the way, Kevin," as he nudged the cat along with his foot. "Toys galore beyond the door, oh yes, I do like that one. A magical feeling with so many toys under one ceiling, that's my other one, yes, yes." Jack realised that this was not the cockney accent that had originally shouted through the door at them.

Colin led them through a tight hallway as the front door slammed shut loudly behind them. He stopped in his tracks suddenly, forcing everyone to lightly bump into each other.

"So, then, boys, what are you after? We're the toy store with so much more. Yes, that's another one of my favourites."

"Weirdo," Jack whispered in Mum's ear. Mum gave him a nudge to shut him up.

"Cluedo, I hear you say." As Colin misheard, Jack almost snorted out loud. "We probably have a dusty version in the warehouse somewhere but I was thinking something more exciting? What do you like? Name me three things. Any things—any toys—your choice—up to you—go for it—come on—what you waiting for? Cat got your tongue? Oh diddly-dum."

"Crazy man," Jack whispered to Mum again, this time drawing one of Mum's looks that didn't need any words to tell him to be quiet.

"Action Man, I hear you say. That's a bit before your time young man but I'm sure we can manage it." This time Jack couldn't hold back and a full-snorted laugh came out. He was actually enjoying the entertainment now and all his anxiety had disappeared.

Colin didn't even batter an eyelid at Jack's reaction. "Come on, then, tell me what you like?"

Charlie piped up, "*Star Wars*, football, monster trucks and cuddly toys."

"Hmmmm, we'll see what we can do," Colin responded. "And you?" he peered at Jack.

"Erm—the same, apart from the cuddly toys."

"Hmmm, interesting." Colin was staring straight through them now, you could see him thinking but he paused in thought for far too long to feel comfortable in the silence.

Dad broke the silence. "Okay, Colin, is Ja-erm—the owner here?" Dad had clearly stopped himself saying something. Jack wondered for a second what it was but soon moved on to thinking about where the hallway was leading them. This was the strangest toy shop he had ever been to, not like Toys R Us.

"Hello, there. I'll take it from here, Colin, thank you." The cockney accent reappeared from the room at the end of the hallway.

"In here, all of you," the voice continued.

Colin piped up like a ringmaster at the circus, "And introducing to you, our special owner and the mind behind this great place—" Jack chuckled again. "James S. Brogan!"

Colin almost pushed all four of the family into the end room where a tall distinguished man, very smart-looking with short, grey hair and a moustache, stood. Charlie thought he looked a very kind man and he couldn't help notice he had the shiniest shoes that he had ever seen, he could see the ceiling lights reflecting in them and he was sure that if he got up close, then he would see his own reflection in them, they were like mirror shoes. The room which he was in was totally different to the dark and dingy hallway; it was bright, airy with high ceilings and large windows. Cream-coloured walls with pictures of some of London's great landmarks. St Paul's Cathedral, Houses of Parliament and Big Ben were three that Jack recognised. As you would expect in a toy shop, there were metres and metres of shelves but they were empty. In fact, the only thing that was filling them was a thick layer of dust that didn't do the rest of the room justice. Where were all the toys? Then, as James S. Brogan stepped forward to shake each one of their hands individually to welcome them, Jack and Charlie caught a glimpse of the mound of toys behind him.

Charlie took five steps towards the pile, jaw dropping further down his chest with each stride. There, lying in front of them were all of the Star Wars vehicles and figures, a radio controlled monster truck, a mound of City football goodies, all you could wish for and about twenty different cuddly toys.

"These," James announced, "are your toys, my little buddies and I can do you a very special discount price. How much do you want to pay for all of these?"

Charlie didn't always understand the value of money. "I'd pay a million pounds for these,"

James laughed and gave a reassuring pat on the head to Charlie.

"How much pocket money have you earned this month?"

"We did loads of jobs this month so we got ten pounds each," Charlie replied enthusiastically.

"Hmmm. Well, you're some way off a million pounds, young man. How about I do you a deal, eight pounds for the lot?"

Now Jack came into the conversation. "Wow, these toys must be worth about six hundred pounds and you want to sell them to us for eight pounds? Why?" The question was spoken with intent and accusation and took James aback, he visually stumbled for words.

"Sale, yes, yes, it's our sale," Colin interrupted. "Our customers are special to us, yes, very special, we like to reward them with great discounts, so, so, do we, erm, do we have a deal?"

"Yes, wicked!" Charlie shouted, over-excited and almost diving into the pile of toys.

"That's eight pounds each so sixteen pounds in total, then," James had moved himself behind the counter and the cash till dinged. This was a deal that was moving at pace.

"Hold on a minute. Mum, Dad, can we have these, please?"

Jack tried to hide the suspicious look from James and Colin; that was aimed at Dad in particular.

"Of course, mate. You can pay us back from your pocket money when we get back home."

"Cash only, sir!" Colin once again interrupted.

"That's fine. Do you want to pay, Jack?" Dad offered the cash to Jack.

"No, you do it." Jack was behaving very warily, quite opposite to his brother who was charming the two shop assistants with his bounciness and innocence. Dad paid over the money. James then whispered something to Dad which Jack didn't catch and then Dad announced that the toys would be delivered to their home when they got back from their trip in a few days' time.

"Oh, can't I stay and play?" Charlie moaned.

"No, we need to get you back and in bed, mate."

Charlie gave an over-exaggerated pout, with his bottom lip nearly hitting the floor.

Mum had managed to hustle all of them together and began herding them out of the shop when James startled them with an almighty shout. "Woah, woah, woah, hold it right there."

Jack knew it. Something bad was about to happen.

"It says here on my till that you are customer number one thousand since the shop opened, which means you have won a fantastic prize." Now he had Jack's attention, he loved winning things. "Please step back in."

"Let's see what he has to say," Mum whispered to the boys.

"You have won an amazing, spectacular and once-in-a-lifetime trip to Disney World in Florida."

"Wow, brilliant. We've already been there," Charlie punched the air in celebration.

"You have won an amazing, spectacular and twice-in-a-lifetime trip to Disney World in Florida," James quipped. This made Jack and Charlie laugh and the exhilaration and excitement crept through them.

"You will fly on my private jet from Heathrow and join up with children from around the world, who have won this great prize from our other shops dotted all over the globe: Sydney in Australia; Tokyo in Japan; Cape Town in South Africa and of course, our flagship store in Greenland. No parents allowed, just a children's holiday of a lifetime."

Jack took a step back. "No parents?" He wasn't sure himself whether it was an excited statement or a cautious question.

"No parents," James unhelpfully just repeated Jack's words.

"No parents?" this time it was a question from Jack.

"No parents," James repeated again.

"Can we?" Jack shot a question directly at Mum.

He expected Mum to say, 'No', straight away, or at least look a little bit taken back that Jack was so taken by the idea of not wanting them there, but she just said, "Let me and your dad have a chat about it," and they disappeared into the corner of the room, muttering, whispering, Mum quite animated, Dad quite still and unmoved.

"We know what answer it will be," Jack said to Charlie but loud enough so that all could hear as if by openly sharing his attitude, it would have an influence over their decision.

"How long?" shouted Dad over to James.

"Just a week," came the instant, sprightly reply.

More muttering and whispering commenced from the corner. Charlie crossed his fingers, his toes and then his legs, which made him look like he needed the toilet.

Mum and Dad's huddle broke up, the low voices ceased and Jack and Charlie had that nervous tightening in their stomachs.

"We have spoken about it," Mum started, "and you are only ten and eight years old, you can do what you like when you are eighteen years old but you are still very young."

Jack huffed and puffed out loud, the red mist descending once more as he awaited the words of disappointment.

"But you have shown us that you are very sensible and, if you promise us that you will look after each other, stay together all of the time and always be close to an adult, then we have decided that you can go."

Jack's mouth gaped open. Charlie was dancing a jig and Colin tried to high five James, drawing an unimpressed look from James as Colin's hand smacked him on his shoulder; it's always hard to high five with only one person interested.

"When do they fly?" asked Dad.

"Next flight is tomorrow morning," James said,

"Tomorrow morning," Charlie said. "But what about our trip to the waxwork museum?"

"What would you rather do, Disney World or see some dummies?" Jack snapped sarcastically. Charlie didn't need to answer.

"When and where?" Mum asked.

"Nine a.m. with passports. Terminal Three at Heathrow. We will meet you in the terminal building near check-in desk thirty-eight."

And that was that. The Crosses strolled out of the shop, Jack and Charlie were on their way to Disney World—without Mum and Dad!

Back at the hotel, Jack had some delayed thoughts. Why were Mum and Dad letting them go? They weren't even allowed on some sleepovers, never mind going to America with strangers. Why hadn't they asked for proof of who James and Colin were? How could Mum and Dad say that their boys were the most precious thing to them and then just allow them to trot off into the sunset like this? How did Mum and Dad know about that toy shop? The owners also had a toy shop in Greenland, really? James had his own private jet just from some dusty old toy shops? Jack lay awake, thinking and thinking, too many thoughts to get to sleep. At three a.m., he began to slowly drift down the tunnel of dreams; sheer exhaustion won against his deep thoughts.

Chapter 5
Take-off

Jack and Charlie heaved their rucksacks across the Heathrow tarmac leading to the only plane that looked like a private jet. It was smaller than the commercial planes but, as Charlie kept on repeating over and over, to Jack's annoyance, "It's posher!"

It had been a strange morning, rushed and hectic, culminating in a very quick hug and kiss from Mum and Dad as the boys made their way through the gates in the departure lounge. Oddly, Mum and Dad seemed unemotional about the boys leaving for a week's holiday without them, almost relaxed about it. They expected at least some visible nerves or even maybe a few held-back tears from Mum, but nothing. Jack was almost disappointed, although it enabled him to enjoy taking charge for at least the walk across the runway.

"Stay with me, Charlie," he bossed. "Stay within the lines else you'll get run over. We don't want to have to fold a flat Charlie into the rucksack."

"That's Mum's joke," Charlie muttered. Jack heard but chose to ignore him and instead concentrated on the very grown-up task of navigating the traffic of luggage wagons that seemed to ignore the zebra crossing markings on the road as they zig-zagged to their destination plane.

They reached the bottom of the plane's steps and stared up at the silver plane with black wings. Just from the outside of the plane, Jack was excited about the luxurious surroundings that awaited them. Mum and Dad would be jealous, they always said they wanted the chance to turn left into business class on a plane rather than the cattle class to the right that they always travelled on.

"Captain Arigo," a voice boomed from behind them. The pilot, in full uniform, held out his hand to them both. Charlie shook it whilst grinning broadly at Jack, not once making eye contact with the pilot, too busy with the hilarity of the situation. Jack sheepishly then followed his little brother by shaking the captain's hand.

"Please climb aboard. Your seats are in the centre of the plane, just past the bedrooms and next to the showers," the captain continued with an assertive but slightly accented tone.

"Bedrooms? Showers?" Charlie repeated to Jack whilst he started to hug his brother in excitement. Jack shrugged him off, unsuccessfully trying to hide his own exhilaration.

As they climbed aboard, they were surrounded by marble tables, brown leather reclining chairs, drinks cabinets that were full of alcoholic and soft drinks and floor-to-ceiling TVs. This was going to be the shortest ten-hour flight ever!

A recognisable voice came from the far end of the plane. "Strap yourselves up, boys, I will come through to you once we have taken off." It was James. The cockney voice was a welcoming noise to Jack's ears, despite not knowing him. A small amount of familiarity seemed to provide some comfort.

Both of the boys took seats at opposite sides of the plane; there were only four seats in their part of the plane anyway but it was nice not to have to argue to see who was going to have the window seat on the way out and who was going to have the window on the way back. Charlie instantly pressed the button to recline his seat and James instantly shouted through politely, "You need your seat in the upright position for take-off, Charlie. After that, put your feet up all you like." Charlie wondered how he knew he had put his feet up, then noticed in each corner of the room was a CCTV camera. Charlie gave a wave and a grin to the camera, Jack joined in the fun with a thumbs up and pulling a face.

James playfully shouted through again "the G-Force might make you stay like that Jack, we are taking off in ten, nine, eight, seven—"

Jack and Charlie steadied themselves and carried on the count. "Six, five, four—"

The jet started picking up speed.

"Three, two, one—WE'RE DOING A WHEELIE, TAKE OFF!" they chorused.

"You've done this before, you two." James was drowned out by the engine noise.

The plane arced around in the sky and then levelled up. Jack's ears popping in the process and temporary deafness consumed him for a couple of minutes.

"Belts off, now for the truth," a well-spoken voice they didn't recognise instructed. They both sharply turned behind them as the new voice entered the room and a short, sharp moment of puzzlement, and then a longer pause of panic came over them as James entered the room.

"Remain calm, remain calm, there is no need to be alarmed," James continued in his very, very posh public school voice. "I know you will find this strange, but this is my real voice and you are not on a flight to Disney World."

"You're kidnapping us," Jack stated with a mix of anger and panic making his voice quiver. Charlie just remained open-mouthed.

"Absolutely not, my friends. I am about to give you the opportunity of a lifetime to do something that boys of your age, in fact, most people, will never, ever experience. I just need you to remain calm and trust me. Everyone on this plane is here for you."

"Calm? Calm? You're kidnapping us," Jack accused James. "I don't suppose your name is even James, is it?"

"Why aren't we going to Disney World?" Charlie innocently raised a question.

"Right, let me start. My name *is* James but it's not James S. Brogan. Just James will do for now. I want to put your minds at rest. Give me just ten minutes to explain and if you are not happy and willing to continue the flight, then we can just turn the plane around and return to Heathrow. I will call your mum and dad and they can pick you up."

Despite the circumstances, Jack felt reassured by James and calmed down fairly quickly, which tended to go against his natural instinct.

"Continue." Jack had learned that one word can often have a bigger impact than a number of words, from his experiences of being told off by Mum and Dad. Mum used the 'continue' line when either of the boys needed to explain their actions, normally very quickly!

"Yes, continue," Charlie copied his brother with a smile, not really grasping the severity of the situation.

Jack looked down at his watch and pressed the stopwatch button. "You have ten minutes from now," although he had no idea what he would be able to do if James over-ran on the ten minutes or he didn't like what he told them.

"I like your style," James commenced. "You are on an unmarked plane for Her Majesty's Secret Service. Not just the secret service but the most secret service." James elongated the pronunciation on 'the' and 'most' for dramatic effect. Jack and Charlie sat, stunned, not moving but still listening.

James carried on. "You are in the safest of hands, as long as nothing that I share with you now goes beyond us." He didn't wait for a response or reply and continued with the confidence that the boys would agree. "Have you heard of MI6, the UK's Secret Intelligence Service – or SIS, as they are known?"

Jack and Charlie just stared straight at him, still stunned.

"I'll take that as a 'yes'. Well, we are MI60. You will have not have heard of us, If you have, then we have failed. We are the most secret of secret services. Only the Queen, the prime minister and the small command structure at MI60 are aware of us. That is no more than seven people in the world, now nine, including you. Even the pilot flying this plane has no idea of our existence, it's on a 'need to know' basis and you need to know. Any questions up to now?"

Jack and Charlie had still not recovered and just blinked and looked back with blank expressions on their faces so James continued.

"We have had a recent incident where our existence was nearly uncovered by one of our mission targets, or in civilian language, our enemy. We have to look at new and innovative ways of carrying out our missions, with some of our agents being placed at risk due to this incident. We can no longer use them. This is where you come in. What is more secret than a secret service which no-one will ever suspect? A secret service using the younger being,—you! Who would suspect two boys of your age being secret agents? Sheer brilliance. Unfortunately, I didn't come up with this brilliance, Her Majesty the Queen had the idea. However, I have had the delight of hand-picking you as our chosen pair."

The boys finally found their tongues.

"You mean us coming to your toy shop wasn't just luck?" Charlie asked.

"No," replied James. "That was all part of a very pleasing plan."

"So Mum and Dad were part of this, then." Charlie was very quickly, maybe too quickly, cut off by James.

"No, your parents were led into this from our Toy Shop advertisements that we sent directly through to them on a number of occasions, through the post and by email. Subliminal messaging, look it up on the internet. That toy shop does not exist, it is just an abandoned room that was convenient for our plan. Remember Colin?" The boys nodded in unison. "He is the head of MI60, my boss. He is also an exceptional actor, don't you think?"

The empty looks returned to the boys' faces. Curious Colin? Surely not?

"You will go on the most amazing adventure that will likely take you to several countries and you will have access to gadgets that you have only seen in the movies. This is your real-life secret agent adventure, your own mission. No other brothers in the whole world will ever have this experience. You are unique, you are special and you will be representing your country."

"You mean like Jimmy Farvey? He represents England," Charlie questioned.

"I assure you that you will be far more important to your country than Jimmy Farvey by the end of this mission," James replied.

If an internal warm glow could be seen by another person, then James was now looking at two beaming boys not just warm with excitement, but boiling over. He had sold it to them.

"But what about our mum and dad?" Jack asked, jolting James out of basking in his perceived glory. "Are you going to ask them first?"

"Your mum and dad think you are in Disney World for a week. Remember what I said. We are the most secret service. My parents think I travel around the world selling computers. Secret means secret. The best adventures are those that are shared by only a small few. I can keep a secret if you can?" James smiled encouragingly to the boys.

"We're in," Jack took charge. Charlie looked up at Jack sharply and Jack put an arm around his shoulder. "Mum and Dad will never know. Let's go on an adventure."

Charlie smiled mischievously and widened his eyes and wiggled his eyebrows to show his expectation for the adventure ahead.

"That's my boys!" James shook them both by the shoulders approvingly.

"Just two questions, James. Why us and what next?" Jack enquired.

"Why you? The bond. You have the most amazing brotherly bond that means you will work together as a team and you will work for each other. There is no point trying to get someone to work for me. I will not be on the ground carrying out the mission. Your loyalty needs to be to each other, not to me. You are close and with closeness comes loyalty.

"What next? You need to go and get your head down and rest. When you wake up, I will show you some real toys, your new gadgets. Whilst you rest, you need to think of an alias. Your first names stay the same, your surname needs to change, it's how it works as a secret agent. Go rest and think in the bedrooms. Boys, we are flying to Mexico!"

Chapter 6
The Preparation

A radio-controlled flying spy camera no bigger than a fly; a watch that contained a GPS tracker, torch, Taser and emergency beacon; a rucksack that converted into a jet pack; heat-seeking rocks that could be thrown with amazing accuracy; ropes that would self-attach to any surface; hidden walkie-talkies that were inserted into the ear. James had started their training three hours later as they flew over the Atlantic Ocean. The boys were introduced to some of the most futuristic and unbelievable gadgets that they had ever seen. Mum and Dad had never let them watch James Bond as 'it had some rude bits in it' so they hadn't even had the opportunity to even see this kind of thing in the movies.

Neither of the boys had slept very well; the adrenaline was pumping, the excitement of an adventure, the nervousness of the unknown, the confusion that these two feelings create when experienced together. James had disturbed their disturbed sleep with the offer of some food. Not just any food, apparently; the diet of spies, wholesome food that kept you going for days on end. Jack and Charlie didn't understand the science behind it but the food was laced with all sorts of chemicals that stretched out the nutritional impact ten times longer than normal, so rather than feeling hungry or lacking in energy after a few hours, it meant that the energy gained from one meal could last for days. This was essential in the line of work they now found themselves in.

As well as having the chance to try out all of the gadgets. (Charlie found it highly hilarious to keep zapping James with his Taser on safe mode and watching the electric shock fling him across the room and seeing him get up with huge sticking-up hair) The boys were also trained in hand-to-hand combat, map reading and first aid. They had made-to-measure camouflage suits produced right in front of them by the on-flight tailor; they had gadget-laden shoes made by the on-flight shoemaker and personalised parachutes with satellite-guided navigation systems attached, made by the on-flight parachute rigger. All the usual services that Jack and Charlie were used to getting at home!

"Right, men—erm—boys. The fun is now out of the way, it's time to get serious." James threw open his arms as if he was talking to a whole audience rather than just the two of them.

"Right, serious. Let's get serious, Charlie." Jack shook Charlie by the shoulders as they both giggled at Jack mimicking James.

"Jack!" the short, sharp tone of James's voice took them both by surprise. "You need to focus, you are no longer in a kid's world. You will be treated as men from this point on. Where you will be going you will be put at risk, you will be pushing yourself to the limits and your country will be relying on you to complete your mission successfully. Do I have your attention?"

Jack nodded and bowed his head like a naughty schoolboy.

"Boys, your mission objective is to collect a package from the Mayan Jungle in Mexico and bring it home to the UK. I can't tell you what is in the package, all that I can tell you is the security of the UK is reliant on the package being delivered safely home. The content of the package is on a 'need to know' basis. However, when I talk about a package, it won't be wrapped in brown paper with sticky tape on it. We use the word 'package' in our world as the word for any target that is moveable. Our past missions have included packages such as gold bars, missiles, rare plants and people. I will not be telling you what the package looks like, as it is for your own protection that you do not know. You will know when you find it, trust me."

"So, let's get this right, we are going on a mission for you, in an unfamiliar country, in a jungle, and you won't even tell us what our target looks like? We might be kids but we're not stupid," Jack retorted.

"That's exactly why we picked you, because you are not stupid. It is for your protection. If you are captured by the enemy, then it is far easier to genuinely deny any knowledge of the target but you will most certainly notice the package when you reach the target location," James reassured him.

"C-c-captured?" Jack stuttered with the realisation now setting in.

"It is always a hazard of the job, I'm afraid, but you are working with the best and we will ensure that no harm comes to you. We have the finest rescue team ready to engage whenever required." This felt strangely reassuring to Jack and he could tell Charlie was up for the adventure.

"Then you have the finest MI60 agents ready to roll, James." Jack puffed out his chest with pride.

"One final thing, your new surname, your new MI60 name. What will it be?" James asked.

Both of the boys had forgotten that James had mentioned the name change earlier. They looked at each other, pulled a strained face to signal that they had forgotten and then Charlie piped up, "Well, Mum always said that we are like a rock wall, so how about Rockwall?"

"The Rockwall Brothers, MI60's finest," Jack announced, staring into the distance as if it was written in the clouds outside of the plane window.

"Jack and Charlie Rockwall, I like it," James agreed. "Now, go and get more rest and food. You will be parachuting out of this plane as we pass over Mexico at exactly oh four hundred hours under the cover of darkness."

That was six hours away. Jack and Charlie, the Rockwalls, high fived each other and made their way to the mound of food laid out on the table at the back end of the jet. They might as well eat, as sleep would be impossible.

Chapter 7
The Mission

"Wooooooooooooooooooaaaaaaaaaah!" Charlie squawked,
"Aaaaaaaaaaaaaaaaaaaarrrrrrgh!" Jack screeched.
They hurtled through the sky at a hundred and twenty miles per hour.
"Keep the noise down, boys, you nearly deafened me, screaming like that." James talked into their ears through their invisible walkie-talkies as they were freefalling from the plane. They both surprised themselves by just jumping from the plane into the darkness below, without hesitation, following James's count down from ten.

Their satellite-guided jumpsuits and parachutes would guide them down from the sky with pinpoint accuracy and land them within twenty feet of each other, despite not being able to see anything at all. It was dark and both of the boys were normally apprehensive of the dark; not scared of the dark, just apprehensive. However, there was too much else to think about as they moved like a blur, heading towards the ground with no idea whether the amazing parachute technology that James had told them about would even work.

Then without warning, an almighty jerk made them feel that they were being dragged back upwards, towards the plane, but it was the automatic release of the parachute which was only slowing down their descent. Bodies recovering from the shock of moving from a hundred and twenty to twenty miles per hour in the space of half a second, hearts beating faster, heads tense from the G-force and the feeling of the cold chill of the cloudless night air despite being about to enter the forty-degree heat of the Mexican jungle.

Then there was calm, a strange tranquillity as they floated effortlessly towards the jungle floor like seagulls free-gliding in the coastal air, the wind passing their ears creating a swishing tunnel of noise like when they opened the car window on the motorway, and finally the sudden realisation that they would have to do some physical work as they touched down on the ground at exactly the same time and their legs whirred round like the cartoon character Road Runner, trying to keep up with the pace of the landing. Jack and Charlie both landed in a heap underneath their parachutes precisely twenty feet apart, as indicated by their new watches that kept track of each other's location.

They both whispered into their watches, "Parachute de-activate," as instructed by James before he counted them down. They seemed to be getting the hang of this professional agent business already! The parachutes immediately folded away into the backs of their jumpsuits but the advanced technology meant that their jumpsuits did not get bulkier or heavier. It was as if the parachute had just disappeared into thin air, Charlie chuckled to himself in amazement.

The noise of the jungle at night instantly hit them, a noise that unless you have experienced it you cannot describe – an eerie atmosphere. It is only at night that you can hear the range of dangerous, venomous and unwelcoming jungle creatures; during the day, the animal world seems so much quieter. It was not only the animals that James had warned them about but the native people, who were not used to visits from outsiders like themselves and they had been told about their blow darts that they used to knock unwanted visitors unconscious. "Avoid them at all costs," James had warned, which Jack felt was strange advice as they clearly wouldn't be shot by the darts on purpose.

"Okay, Charlie?" Jack whispered over to his little brother. No response. "Charlie?" Jack enquired with a bit of urgency in his voice.

"I winked, Jack." The reply came out of the darkness.

"You are such a wally! How am I supposed to see you in this darkness?" Jack replied, exasperated by Charlie's clear stupidity.

"Well, I've put on my sunglasses and I can see you," Charlie said.

"Sunglasses!" Jack's shout broke the quietness with extreme exasperation. "Stop messing around, we haven't got time and I need to find the way in this darkness."

"Put your sunglasses on, Jack," Charlie advised.

"Don't be so stupid," Jack continued to be irritated and felt around in the dark to grab his brother by his jumpsuit. "Come here and stop being an idiot, these are clearly not going to make you see in the dark," as he whipped off his brother's sunglasses in an annoyed state and put them to his eyes.

"See?" Charlie stood firm.

"Ah. I wasn't to know," Jack refused to apologise.

"Night vision sunglasses," a voice came over their communication system. It was James. "Use them at all times in the dark and you will be able to see as clear as day, another one of our many gadgets that we have developed over the last five years."

Jack threw the sunglasses back at Charlie and reached into the pocket of his jumpsuit for his own pair. He hated being wrong. Charlie smugly put the sunglasses back on and muttered under his breath sarcastically, "That's okay, Jack, no need to say sorry." Jack just shot him one of his looks.

"You need to head north-west through the thick jungle growth for about three miles, as we previously discussed. Beware of the natives but also be aware of the local gangs that patrol this region, they will be expecting trouble at some point because of the package that they hold. Use your gadgets wisely. I will stop communication to avoid distracting you. You are on your own for a bit but I will be following you through the satellite tracking. All clear?"

"Yes," Jack responded.

"Yes, affirmative," Charlie stated.

"Then good luck, boys, do your country proud," James signed off.

Jack and Charlie studied their surroundings for a few seconds and then, without further word, began to follow the north-westerly directions given by James. They used their machete knives to cut through the vines, long grass and branches to pave the way. They continued in silence for about two miles, thinking about the task ahead but also keeping a watchful eye out for other people. A loud, cracking branch made them stop suddenly. They both stooped to minimise their visibility and listened intently. After a few seconds, a small wild cat passed through. Charlie recognised the cat from watching Steve Backshall shows; it was a margay, harmless to humans but deadly for small animals. Charlie signalled to Jack to carry on and they rose as one as the wild cat passed by without even looking at them. They had only taken five more steps when there was an almighty breakout of shouting in a foreign voice. "Intrusos más aquí!" Jack and Charlie didn't have time to activate their translation gadget but it sounded like the voices were not friendly and coming directly for them, at speed!

Barking dogs, torch lights and what sounded like about ten men's voices all shouting aggressively. "Let's run in the direction we're heading but stay close together, do not get split up," Jack instructed and they set off, racing to their target. They remained calm despite the clear danger. As their increased speed made greater noise, the voices began to identify their location and headed towards them, increasing their own pace at the same time. Their voices seemed to get more excitable and angry.

They were closing on them. The Rockwalls needed to think quickly, think of a diversion plan to send the voices in a different direction. Charlie started rummaging through his backpack, trying to find a gadget that could help. "Got it," he announced. "Jack, carry on running, I'm going to divert them."

Jack actually did as he was told for once, confident that his brother could deal with the situation.

"I'll meet you at the target location in ten minutes. If you are not there, then I will use the tracking system to locate you."

Jack burst into an even faster sprint while Charlie huddled down with his gadget.

It was a hologram bomb. Once exploded, it created a fake 3D image of whatever the user chose; all it needed was a voice-activated instruction and then it would explode within ten seconds. Charlie pulled the pin on the hand grenade-looking weapon and spoke into the in-built microphone. "Bomb crater, activate." he swiftly put the bomb down, picked up his rucksack and ran in the same direction as Jack.

Boom, the noise rippled around the jungle. Birds flew into the night sky, animals scampered for cover. The voices headed towards the explosion and were met with a scene from a disaster movie – burnt trees, tree stumps on fire, a ring of flames around a bomb crater about a half a mile wide. None of it real, just a hologram, they could walk straight through it but it would take a good half an hour for them to realise it. The distraction should see the brothers get well ahead of their pursuers. The angry shouts of the men reverberated around the jungle, "Los hemos perdido!" Charlie pressed his translator, "We've lost them!" the computerised voice translated into his ear.

Charlie punched the air. "Yes! Come on!" He could see Jack squatting down next to an opening in the trees and he ran up alongside him and knelt down.

"Well done, mate," Jack grinned, clearly proud of his brother's work. "Look through there," he pointed through to a clearing in the jungle undergrowth. There, standing before them was the most amazing pyramid that they had ever seen, although to be honest, it was the first one they had seen apart from on the television. They had watched documentaries about the Egyptian pyramids and they had had topic talks at school about them but this pyramid was different. It was grey rather than sand-coloured; it had a flat top with what looked like a ruined temple on top; it had over-sized steps up the centre of the sloped sides leading to the temple and an entrance door at the summit. Despite the pyramid being in the clearing, it was obvious that it had previously been covered in the vines found across the whole jungle as the remains of severed vines were attached to the outside of the pyramid. Jack assumed that the vines had been chopped away at some point.

The boys looked in awe. "This is our target location, according to my watch." Jack pushed his watch in front of Charlie's face to accentuate the point.

"What now? How do we get in there, then? Those men must be guarding this place and they will probably be here in about twenty minutes. We have no idea what to expect once we are out in the open," Charlie quizzed Jack.

"We are the country's elite agents. I guess we just head for the only way into the place, through the front door," Jack nodded his head towards the door at the top of the pyramid.

"Simples!" Charlie grinned.

"On my count of three, we go together, straight up the steps and let's hope the door is not locked, got it?" Jack asked.

"Got it," Charlie agreed.

Jack commenced the count "One, two—"

"Wait, wait," Charlie interrupted. "Here's a smoke bomb to cover our movements, then no-one can see us directly."

"Good idea. Here we go. One, two, three," Jack finished the count. Charlie threw the smoke bomb in front of them as they ran and the smoke drifted with them as they headed towards the steps of the pyramid. As they reached the steps, it became clear that they would be too large for them to climb like normal steps. Jack reached into his bag and pulled out a bow and arrow, pointed it at the top step and let the arrow fly. A rope was attached to the arrow and as the arrow embedded itself in the mortar between the pyramid blocks, Jack fired another arrow into the bottom step, making the rope taut and providing a way to shimmy up the pyramid. The rope was now the boys' only chance of getting to the top of the steps. There was no sign of the men chasing them but how long would that last?

Jack jumped on the rope, flung himself upside down and started to pull himself up the rope like a monkey up a pole. Charlie followed suit. It was hard going but the boys had plenty of climbing experience as they went to After School Club at the local Outdoor Pursuits Centre every Thursday. Climbing and abseiling were two of their favourite activities; this combined the two skills.

The first signs of light were beginning to poke through the jungle wilderness so it was a good job the smoke screen that they had created was still hanging around in the air. In no time at all, both boys had reached the summit with no incidents, although the rope was a little bit wobbly and creaky with the two of them climbing on it at the same time. As they disembarked from the rope, Jack took out his machete and cut it, winding it in to use again at another point. He kept one end attached to the arrow as he chipped it out of the mortar with the tip of the machete. He stuffed it in his rucksack and pushed the button on the side which sucked the contents together and put the bag back to its usual size and weight. They were both beginning to get used to the amazing gadgets that they had been trusted with.

Charlie gave the door a light push to see whether it was open. It didn't move.

Jack whispered, "Push it harder."

Charlie gave it a more solid push and the door moved but instead of it opening at the hinges, it began to fall inwards from the top and with a loud thump, the door hit the floor. Throwing up a puff of dust, it lay flat out. Charlie looked at Jack, Jack looked at Charlie, Charlie raised his arms and flexed his biceps and out loud made a, "Boof, boof, boof," sound, just as his dad always did to mess around to make them laugh, like he was a bodybuilder. Jack and Charlie belly-laughed.

They looked out across the jungle at the first light of the day appearing beyond the thickness of the jungle growth and trees. The view of the sunrise from the top of the pyramid was stunning. However, they drew deep breaths as they were about to enter into the unknown of the darkness within the pyramid. They ducked into the doorway, leaving the distant voices and the comfort of the outdoors behind them.

Chapter 8
The Forgotten World

Darkness but the feeling of not being alone, the exhilaration of being chased, not knowing what you are being chased into, inexperience of the situation, how could this have any other outcome than a catastrophic outcome? The answer? Gadgets.

"Room light," instructed Jack. A glow came from the back of his rucksack that lit the breadth and height of the inside of the pyramid. Darkness sorted.

"Hologram bomb number two." Charlie threw the hologram bomb at the empty door frame where the door had been before he had shoved it inwards. A new holographic door grew out of nothing and a crevice in the ground, the width of a large house, appeared in front of their eyes. The chasing pack was going to be held up even further.

"Virtual map," demanded Jack. A 3D map appeared on the ground ahead of them showing the layout of the immediate vicinity and the surrounding area. Who said they didn't know where they were?

Inexperienced? The boys were behaving like true professionals, like professional secret agents.

They took in their new surroundings, pretty much what you would expect from a building that was over one thousand years old – dark, dusty and a smell that gave them the impression that no-one had inhabited the pyramid for that length of time!

The boys cast their eyes around the inside of the pyramid without moving. The room, if you could describe it as a room, was just one cavernous space but there was something strange. There was nothing in it. It was just a big, dusty, grey, featureless, empty space. No historical markings, no treasures, no sign of recent life and unlikely to have been a hideout for a gang of natives hiding a package of national interest to the UK. There were also no other doors apart from the one they had just come through. That was a problem as they would have to face the pursuit team that were on their trail, just to get back out of the pyramid.

The boys instinctively split up without saying a word to each other and began to explore, Jack checking the walls going anti-clockwise and Charlie going clockwise. They were just grimy, grey stone walls that had clearly had the jungle vines ripped from their frontage. This was the only sign that others had trodden the same path where Jack and Charlie were currently treading.

As Charlie ran his hand along the walls almost with boredom as there was nothing else to look at, he broke the silence. "What shall we do now, Jack? There's nothing here. Maybe there's another pyramid a few miles on? Shall we go and check it out?" Charlie leant against a block of stone that protruded from the pyramid wall.

Jack swivelled to face Charlie and started to talk at the same time. "I don't kn—" he stopped in his tracks. "Charlie? Charlie! Charlie! Where are you?" His heart once again racing, Jack speedily made his way to where he last heard his brother speaking to him.

"Charlie! Charlie!" His voice echoed from wall to wall. All he could see was the solid, grey wall.

"Charlie!" No response.

Jack began to talk to himself. "Right, think, the satellite watch." He looked at his watch that was showing that his brother was right here in the spot where he stood. "Useless." He aimed the insult at his watch as if it would make a difference to its effectiveness.

"Charlie!" Still no answer.

Jack took off his backpack and sat down on the protruding stone, where he last saw Charlie, to see which gadget might help him in this situation. No sooner had he sat down on the stone than he was falling backwards into a hole that had opened up behind the stone, his backpack hooked around his foot as he seemed to fall for ages, sliding down a stone tunnel, a steep descent and then landing in a heap on a pile of stone rubble.

"Aaah." Jack winced from the pain.

"Don't be such a wimp," a voice came back. Charlie was standing over his brother with a smirk on his face. He put out his hand and hauled his brother out of the stones. Jack brushed himself down and tried to also brush off his brother's remark, scrunching up his face to hide the pain.

"What is this place?" Jack questioned out loud.

"The end of our mission," announced Charlie as he pointed to a stone table in the middle of the room.

There on the table was the most amazing, golden treasure box, just like out of a fictional adventure story.

"The next challenge of our mission," Charlie continued as he pointed to the snakes that were slithering around the stone table like a moat of water protecting a castle.

"Agkistrodon," Jack stated drily.

"No time for talking nonsense, Jack, those bad guys will be along soon to get us," Charlie replied.

"No, Agkistrodon," Jack pointed at the snakes. "One of the most venomous species of snake in Mexico. They can jump great lengths and one bite from the viper can kill you within minutes. Our mission is not yet complete, little bro."

Luckily, the snakes were in a high-sided pit that meant they could not get out, but the pit surrounded the stone table in a circular shape so the only way to get to the treasure box was through the snake pit. An impossible task unless they had a death wish.

The boys looked around their new surroundings to see whether anything could help. It was very much similar surroundings to the previous room, apart from the vines had not been removed from this room, they hung everywhere and covered all of the ceiling and walls. Whoever occupied the pyramid clearly didn't want to spend any time with these slippery companions, they hadn't taken much care with keeping this room in shape.

Jack started to again look through his backpack. "There must be a gadget in here somewhere, something that can either build a bridge over the pit, catapult us over there or provide us with protection from the snakes so we can walk through."

Charlie continued to stare all around the room, contemplating a plan, trying to think quickly.

Jack continued to talk to himself. "Taser, no good; helicopter camera, no; bow and arrow, not this time. There's nothing."

"Jack?" Charlie interrupted

"Not now, Charlie, I'm concentrating," Jack snapped.

"I have a pla—" Charlie was interrupted by Jack.

"Not now, Charlie," Jack shouted. "Maybe if I look further down the rucksack, then there will be something there." Jack shuffled through the bag with no joy.

"Weeeeeeeeeeeeeeeee, I'm flyiiiiiiiiiing!" Charlie squealed at the top of his voice.

Jack shot his head up out of his backpack to catch Charlie swinging from the vines like Tarzan. He swung on one vine, then as it reached its peak, he jumped on to the next one. He swung straight over the snakes then let go and landed like a cat, on all fours, right on the table in the middle of the island. He picked up the treasure box, which wasn't as heavy as he thought it would be, held it up in the air like the League Trophy and shouted, "Got it," to Jack.

"Wicked, well done, dude!" Jack said proudly as Charlie danced a celebratory jig on top of the table.

"Right, how do I get back?" Charlie asked Jack. Clearly, only having thought through half of the plan.

"You wally, Charlie, you shouldn't have let go of the vine," Jack responded unsupportively.

"These snakes look a bit angry with me." Charlie peered over the edge of the table at the reptiles. All of a sudden the pit didn't seem as deep as he had originally thought.

"I will have to swing across. You keep hold of the box and I will pick you up and swing back over, got it?" Jack instructed.

"Got it," Charlie replied.

Jack climbed on to the biggest stone in the room, tested a couple of the vines to ensure they would take his weight and chose the most suitable one. He then leapt.

Slight miscalculation. Jack was a lot taller than Charlie and as he jumped from the first to the second vine, he realised that his legs would be dragging through the snake pit at a height where the snakes could bite him. He instantly pulled his legs up, almost wrapping them around his own neck. The snakes sensed an opportunity and began to snap their bodies upwards at Jack overhead; it was almost like they were standing on the tips of their tails with extra effort to try and inject their lethal venom into his trailing leg.

For the first time, Jack felt the heat of the jungle as his body temperature increased as the adrenaline pumped around his body. One of the snakes managed to catch on to the bottom of his trousers, clinging by a thread with its fangs. Jack, in blind panic, started to fling his legs all over the place trying to shake the snake off; the snake just clung on comfortably. Then 'thwack', the snake disappeared. Charlie had picked up a small rock and thrown it with pinpoint accuracy to knock the snake off. A quick fist pump in the air from Charlie and Jack landed on the table, keeping hold of the vine. "Hold tight." He grabbed hold of Charlie. Jack, Charlie and the treasure box swung back over, Charlie stuck his tongue out at the snakes as he passed over them. The snakes hissed their tongues back at him.

"Phew, that was a close call," Jack said as he got his breath back.

"Let's have a look in the box," Charlie suggested. He eyed up the box where there was a lock, ironically with three golden snakes curling their way around the key hole. There was no sign of a key though and no way into the box without a key.

Jack caught movement in the shadows of the room, someone was there. Then he heard a 'phwwwwt' sound pass his ear. He turned to look at Charlie and saw the blow dart catch him in the neck. Another 'phwwwwt' and both boys were out for the count, knocked unconscious!

Chapter 9
Skyscraping

"Rooooockwaalls, come in." A distant, broken voice echoed around Charlie's head. "Rockwalls, come in," the voice becoming clearer. "Rockwalls, are you receiving?" The voice now so crisp, as if it was a person talking directly into his ear. Charlie stirred. A sore, banging head. Disorientated, dizzy, blurry vision, cold but covered in sweat. He slowly raised himself from the floor, took in the unfamiliar surroundings and then panic. Where was Jack? Where were they? The pyramid? The treasure box? The man in the shadows?

"Rockwalls, come in!"

"James?" Charlie sharply responded.

"Charlie, finally, we've been trying to make contact for the last twenty-four hours, what have you been up to?" James said accusingly but with a huge amount of relief in his voice.

"I —I don't know," Charlie replied, still trying to get his head around where he was and what had happened. "I really don't know. Where am I?"

"Look out of the window," James instructed.

"There are no windows," Charlie observed.

"Look up," James said impatiently.

There, high up at the top of the wall, was a thin slit of a window. Charlie moved the only bit of furniture in the room to stand on; an old, tatty-looking office chair which had clearly had better days. The foam on the seat pad had holes picked into the foam by its owner but it would elevate Charlie to peek out of the window on his tiptoes. He craned his neck up and allowed his eyes to focus on the view and there before him was the most amazing sight. The Empire State Building.

"New York," Charlie whispered to himself in amazement, forgetting that James could hear him.

"That's right, my boy!" James almost sounded happy but Charlie put it down to the post-relief reaction.

"Where's Jack?" Charlie shot a question at James.

"He's safe but in captivity, like yourself, but first of all tell me what happened." James was very directive.

Charlie spent the next five minutes telling James about the pyramid, finding 'the package' and his last memory of trying to unlock the box.

"Okay, we have to be quick now. We can't let your captors hear you talking to me, they will instantly know you are a secret agent. They are dangerous people. Jack is in the next room to you, according to the GPS. Your rucksacks are also in the same room. It is essential you release Jack and you take the rucksacks. Your captors will have looked through the rucksacks and all they will have found is some food, some blank paper and a pen. The gadgets will have been automatically stored safely inside the secret compartment, it will have been triggered by the emergency response that works from your heart rate. No time to go into the science of it but they should be in one piece, just state the command, "Rucksack re-set," into your watch when the rucksack is back on your back and all will be back to normal. Then, you are to recover the package," James continued.

"Normal? Nothing's normal," Charlie queried.

"Forget that, do you understand?" James snapped.

"Yes, affirmative," Charlie confirmed.

"Okay, from this point you are on your own," James announced.

"Before you go, how do I get out of the room? I don't have any gadgets so can't pick the lock," Charlie asked.

"Charlie, you are a secret agent, work it out!" and with that James was gone.

Charlie stared at the door, looked around the room, and turned the chair upside down, expecting to find a key taped to the underside. Maybe climb out of the window? But it was too thin even for his slender body. Maybe he could pull the arm off the chair and use it as a lever to wrench the door open? He would need a tool to get the arm off the chair in the first place. Maybe he could punch a hole in the ceiling and climb through to the next room that way? The ceiling was too high to reach, even using the chair as a step-ladder. That was it, he was out of ideas.

Charlie walked over to the door, stared at it again, leaned his back up against it and slid down it in frustration to slump to the floor. But as he slid down it, his arm caught on the door handle and the door swung ajar, even with Charlie's weight against it. The door was unlocked all along. Charlie gave it the, 'boof, boof, boof,' bicep flex once again, this time with no audience whatsoever but he was a secret agent, they do cool things like that!

He peeked out of the door, looking both ways, almost expecting an armed guard. No-one to be seen, just a magnolia-coloured corridor with a 1950s New York landscape photo hanging immediately in front of him.

He looked both ways again. At the far end to the left was a door; there was nothing to the right apart from the corner of the corridor. He decided to try the door first. Jack could have been in another room to the right but he was sure James would have been more precise with his instructions if that was the case.

Charlie's first step in to the corridor brought the loudest of creaks from the floorboards, it almost made him jump. It probably was not as loud as it sounded in his head, due to him being overly aware of keeping quiet, but it was definitely loud enough to gain attention from whoever they were up against. He carried on regardless, making his way to the dark green door with paint flaking off it and placed his ear against the door. He heard a voice but it was a foreign voice that he couldn't understand; the only words that were remotely familiar were, "Wek up Ingleeeesh," which he broadly recognised as, "Wake up, English." That must be Jack he is talking to, Charlie thought.

Charlie noticed a small crack in the grain of the wood on the door. The door was so old that the crack had been left for a long time and it was wide enough to see the light of the room behind it. He removed his ear from the door and placed his eye at the V-shaped crack. He could see a large window and glimpses of someone moving around. Then lying in the corner he could see Jack lying on the two rucksacks as if they had made him nice and comfortable for a long night's sleep.

"Wekky wekky, Ingleeesh boy," the voice repeated and he saw the man shake Jack. He couldn't really make out any features of the man as he was standing too close to the door. That triggered an idea.

Charlie had a flashback to the quick training that James had given them. He had said to them, "Remember, even boys of your size can do amazing things that you think can only be achieved by older, stronger and more experienced people than yourselves. Always look for the weakness, focus on it and then respond." It was a bit of a cryptic message at the time and he had a vision of him and Jack looking at each other and just shrugging, as if it was just another thing that they would never understand, or not until they were older and wiser. But he began to piece together a plan based on the weaknesses. The weakness did not have to be a person. In this case, he was thinking that the old, rotten door might be the weakness that would become his strength.

Deep breath, exhale, nerves under control. Charlie knocked on the door, took five strides back from the door and waited until he heard the voice.

"Si?" Silence followed.

"Si?" The voice got louder, Charlie remained silent.

"Hola," the voice, now irritated without a reply.

This was his opportunity, he ran and launched a karate kick at the hinges of the door, and the door immediately gave way and the door and Charlie's weight landed right on top of the voice on the other side. Charlie fully expected a tussle but the man was lying under the door, clearly knocked unconscious from the surprise attack. Kerchow! The plan couldn't have gone any better. No time for a boof, boof, boof moment though.

He got straight down on the floor. Jack was asleep. He tried to wake him; no luck. He saw a vase on top of a cupboard that was half full of dull-coloured water, but it was still water and would do the trick. Jack woke with a splutter as Charlie threw the vase's dirty contents across his face. The splutter was then replaced with the same pained expression that Charlie had awoken with only ten minutes before. Not an expression that meant he had had a nice relaxed sleep but one that said that he had been drugged by a poisonous dart for the last few hours.

"Charlie? What happened?" Jack mumbled with a tired-sounding voice.

"Hi, Jack, guess where we are?" Charlie responded. "New York!" he continued without waiting for a reply and as if he was announcing a big holiday to his brother.

"What? York? No, New York? England or America?" Jack replied all confused.

"New York, the Big Apple," Charlie confirmed.

Jack's blurry eyesight began to settle down and he started to take in his surroundings. "What happened to the door? Who's that?" he quickly switched his attention from the damaged door to the unconscious stranger.

Charlie mischievously moved over to the man who was lying underneath the fallen door, with his whole body covered by the wood but his head was poking out from the top of the door. He pulled his chin down and moved his mouth open and shut as he put on a funny voice and made the man into his ventriloquist's dummy. "Hi, Jack, my name's Lazy Larry. I've just lain down here under this door for a little snooze. Don't wake me up else I'll turn in to my alter ego, Angry Harry. You wouldn't like me then."

Charlie then started making snoring sounds as he opened the man's mouth wide. Charlie's clowning around soon brought Jack around from his own drowsiness as they rolled around on the floor in laughter.

Charlie spent a couple of minutes bringing Jack up to speed with his conversation with James and how he had karate kicked the door down, as they looked out of the large window in the room at the Empire State Building. At the same time, Charlie showed Jack how to re-set the rucksacks. Jack peered in to his rucksack and a glimmer of gold caught his eye. To his amazement, he pulled out the treasure box, the package. Why would they leave it within his reach? Maybe they didn't plan on them trying to escape? What if it wasn't the treasure box they were after and was actually them? Why bring them to New York? No answers, though.

"How shall we get out, Jack?" Charlie broke Jack's silent thoughts.

"Well, we have no idea of the corridors and number of floors in this building and who else is accompanying Lazy Larry. The safest way normally would be the stairs but we're secret agents, so the obvious way is out of that window." Jack pointed to the window that had an opening section to it.

Charlie sidled up to the window, gazed downwards, looked back at Jack with a resigned expression on his face. "Fifty floors up. Which one are you going to be, Superman or Batman?"

"Neither, let's be Jet-men," Jack tapped his backpack.

"Jet packs!" Charlie shouted excitedly.

"Shhhhhh," Jack pushed his finger against his lips, eyes wide open.

Lazy Larry let out a murmur from under the door.

"Quick, do as I show you. Activate jet pack," Jack instructed. His backpack, which was already hoisted on to his back, morphed into what appeared to be a jet engine like on an aeroplane. "Then, all you have to do, according to James, is say the same instruction again, once you have jumped out of the window."

"How do you know it will work?" Charlie queried.

"We don't," Jack said nonchalantly, with a shrug.

Lazy Larry began to move his limbs, feeling around without opening his eyes as if he was trying to guess his surroundings just from the sense of touch.

"We've got to move fast," Charlie said as he pulled on his backpack and followed the same routine as Jack.

In the meantime, Jack had opened the window and the realisation of how high up they were hit him. He felt the adrenaline begin to kick in again.

"Qué?" Larry spoke and began to drag himself out from under the door.

"Let's go, go, go," Jack shouted. "Follow me!"

He checked to make sure Charlie was ready; he was. Jack pulled himself up onto the window sill and caught the man, just about making some sense of his situation and ready to pounce on them from across the room. He jumped into the wind, shouted, "Activate jet pack," and the engine kicked in.

Charlie vaulted on to the window sill just as Larry lunged at him. In the same clumsy move, he knocked Charlie straight out of the window and Charlie was falling head first down from the fifty floors. He would have to turn his body around in the air, or else his jet pack would send him at a quicker speed straight into the ground. Ten floors, twenty floors, thirty floors, the ground was coming up to meet him at speed, the yellow cabs getting nearer and nearer. He fought against the strong wind and managed to get his head pointing sideways. "Activate jet pack."

The effect was instantaneous. Charlie was all of a sudden like a—well, a jet plane. He swooped around the sky as the little people below gazed upwards and pointed. He saw Jack in the distance, doing loop the loops in the sky over Madison Square Garden as the crowds gathering for the New York Rangers ice hockey match looked on in amazement. At this moment, these secret agents were not being so secret.

Charlie pointed towards Jack and jetted past the New Yorker Hotel with its prominent neon sign. The faces in the Tick Tock Diner next door peered out of the window to see the 'jet boys' in action. He met Jack at the peak of his loop and managed to stretch out a hand to high five him. Then, an unfriendly face came into view on the ground. Lazy Larry had made his way down to the street and was on his phone, appearing to shout instructions to someone about the whereabouts of the boys. That was the Rockwalls' cue to end the show. Jack gave Charlie a signal to follow him and they headed up into the sky, above the skyscrapers and away from prying eyes.

New York appeared very different from this height; the hustle and bustle in the streets was replaced with a strange serenity. The hum of the crowds and the honking from the yellow cabs could still be heard but almost as a muffled, distant noise. It was a lot colder at this altitude but the excitement of the moment kept the boys warm.

"This way," Jack hollered to Charlie.

"What? I can't hear you over this jet engine!" Charlie shouted back.

Jack flew closer to Charlie. "This way, head for the river. If we split up, at least anyone following us won't be able to follow us both. I know there are some piers there, I saw it in Dad's travel adventure magazine. There is an empty pier, Pier Fifty-seven. Meet you there, be safe."

Charlie gave a wink to his big brother. "Be safe, Bro, and keep that treasure box safe as well." This is fun, Charlie thought to himself, out on my own. He jetted off over the Rockefeller Center and towards the Hudson River, leaving Jack trailing in his wake.

Chapter 10
Hudson Heroics

Jack had spent the last ten minutes trying to find the best way to the edge of the Hudson River. He had flown past some of the most iconic sites; Central Park, Macy's department store, the lights of Times Square and Trump Tower (voted Jack and Charlie's funniest named building).

Finally, he found the Hudson and brought himself to land right next to the Hudson Line Sightseeing Tours building where there were queues of tourists waiting to board their river trips to the Statue of Liberty, the Brooklyn Bridge and seeing the infamous New York City landscape from the water. There was a buzz and murmuring that you only get from people being on holiday, a relaxed, laid back feel despite being in one of the busiest cities in the world. The buzz and noise level seemed to rise when Jack landed right next to them with his jet engine on his back and instructed his backpack to de-activate the jet pack. The engine just disappeared into his bag, right in front of the watching audience. Jack wasn't sure whether he was managing this undercover operation too well, although he enjoyed having an audience and showing off his gadgets.

Quick stop for food; a chilli dog from one of the on-street sellers with tomato ketchup (that's 'toe-may-toe' to those wanting to practise being American) and sauerkraut. Delicious! It was not needed, as the special food that James had laid on for them was keeping the energy levels high, but still delicious. He then sat on a seat next to the Hudson to consider his next steps. He hoped Charlie had found the pier okay but he wanted to ensure that they kept apart for a bit so any followers were avoided.

Jack caught a glimpse of a suspicious man who was dressed in a large blue mack with his collar up and a large floppy hat, almost as if he didn't want his face to be seen. He had a copy of the *New York Times* and was heading directly towards Jack. Jack sat up straight, alert and ready to run. He felt around to his back to ensure his rucksack was secure in case he did have to run. The man continued striding towards him. There was something reassuringly familiar about him, but Jack knew he couldn't afford to be lured into a false sense of security. The man switched the newspaper from his right hand to his left hand, the side nearest to Jack and as he approached and nearly passed him, he dropped the newspaper into Jack's lap and in a fake American accent he blurted out, "Page eight." Despite the fake accent, Jack was certain he had come across the man before. He made a mental note of his clothes and appearance; average size, about five foot ten, a hint of dark but greying hair under a ghastly orange floppy hat, blue mack, blue jeans and white trainers (or sneakers as they called them over here).

Jack soon put the man out of his head, he needed to concentrate. He turned to page eight of the New York Times. It had a page pasted in to the paper with only a few words on it; "Cargo Ship, Pier eight, eight forty a.m. tomorrow morning. Beware of men in all black uniforms."

This wasn't happening to him, it felt like this was something out of a Tin Tin adventure. Maybe it would be made into a movie of their real life adventures; *Rockwall Brothers, the Movie*. At the moment, though, staying alive, getting back to England and keeping out of more trouble was the main aim – the Hollywood career could come after.

Should he trust the man or was this a set-up? Who was he and why was he so familiar? Where was the cargo ship going? Jack tore the page out of the newspaper folded it up and put it in his backpack with the 'package'.

No sooner had Jack thrown the remaining newspaper in the bin than he looked round to see a man dressed all in black approaching him from his left. He turned to begin running to his right, but a man dressed exactly the same was moving at pace towards him with a menacing look on his face. The only way out was back towards the city centre but, no, another man all in black was running and was about a hundred yards away from him in that direction; he was surrounded. That left one option only, the water. This was not how Jack had envisaged his first experience of the Hudson River. He had thought it would be on a family holiday, maybe on one of the Sightseeing Cruises. He had read one of the signs whilst eating his chilli dog, The Freedom Cruise taking in the Statue of Liberty was his preferred choice and he had imagined returning here with Mum, Dad and Charlie in the future. But for now, he prepared himself to get wet.

He secured his rucksack as he sprinted to the bank of the river. He jumped over the barriers of the Hudson Line Pier with a shout and yells from the staff working there. He had to ignore them but he hoped they would understand if they knew his situation. He continued running along the pier, glancing back at the three men in black who were gaining ground on him, especially with the burden of a rucksack and a solid gold treasure box in tow. Just as he was reaching the end of the pier he noticed two speedboats, engines running but no-one in the first of the boats. The second one had two people who looked like they were about to pull away from shore for some private sightseeing of their own. Split second decision. Jack decided to try his hand at driving a speedboat, surely it couldn't be that hard?

He ran and jumped into the captain's seat. This time there were shouts from all around; the people in the boat behind, the men in black and the security guard who had joined the chase. Jack ignored them all, focused on the job.

He pulled back the throttle lever and to his surprise, he was immediately pulling away from the pier, just in time as one of the men in black made a leap from the shore to try to jump on the boat but the gap was too wide and he fell straight into the water. Heart racing, Jack peered over his shoulder to see the other two men in black throwing the two people in the other speedboat into the water, they hijacked their boat and now they were in hot pursuit of Jack.

It is strange how you notice the smallest detail at the most unusual times. Jack noticed that the boat was called the *Lucky Boy*, he hoped this was an omen.

The *Lucky Boy* being captained by the lucky boy was now bouncing off the whippy current on the Hudson, it seemed like the boat was spending more time in the air than actually on the water but he needed the speed to get away from the men in black.

The wind was whipping in Jack's face and was blowing his hair all over the place. No time for vanity though, survival was the focus. He was passing the pleasure cruisers, one after another; people were taking photos of him in the speedboat, not because they knew what was happening but people seemed to be taking photos of absolutely everything that was around them. One man was leaning over the side of a cruise boat and taking a picture of the rusty old anchor on the side. Jack felt sad for his family who would have to put up with seeing those boring photos when he arrived back from wherever he had come from.

Despite being on full throttle, the men in black were gaining on him. All of a sudden, there was a whistling sound past his ear; what was that? Then, another one and another one. They were shooting at him, real bullets. He instinctively ducked his head down a bit further and one bullet pinged off the metal steering wheel on the speedboat; close shave. He had to do something quickly as one of those bullets would hit him very soon. U-turn required!

Jack slowed the speedboat down, turned the steering wheel full lock to the right and then pushed on the full throttle. The boat turned a hundred and eighty degrees, almost on the spot. There were stunned expressions on the faces of the men in black, to all of a sudden have another speedboat heading directly at them at full speed. They began to fire gun shots at Jack rapidly, trying to slow down the approach, Jack ducked even further down, knowing that he just had to keep the boat steady and heading in the right direction. It was going to be a head-on collision, did Jack know what he was doing?

The men in black tried to turn their boat to avoid the clash of steel between the boats but it was too late. Jack shouted, "Activate ejector." His rucksack fired him directly upwards into the air, just as the two boats smashed into each other. A massive explosion lit up the

Hudson and reflected off the glass of the buildings on shore.

The aftermath of the explosion helped take the focus off Jack slowly descending in the air by parachute. As he nearly reached the level of the water, he shouted, "Activate kayak." A blow-up kayak self-inflated and jumped out of the bag then landed on the water. Jack missed the kayak and he had to de-activate the wet parachute and then climb into the kayak soaking wet.

The coastguard and other boats closed in on the scene of the explosion, emergency lights flashing and sirens going. Jack took a deep breath to recover from the moment. However, in that moment, he realised that he did not have a paddle to move the kayak. "Activate paddle," he instructed. Nothing. "Activate oars." Nothing again. "Activate—" he had run out of different words to try.

"These gadgets needs some work on them, this is rubbish," Jack moaned to himself. Only one thing for it. He leaned over the edge and used his arms to propel the kayak forward. He was about half a mile from shore but he was out of the spotlight and he would make his way slowly but surely back to dry land.

Chapter 11
Roof-top Battles

As Charlie looked up, the bright blue sky whizzed by mixed in with the grey of the skyscrapers, it was if the rest of the world was moving around him at two hundred miles per hour, not his jet engine propelling him through the polluted air of the city. He didn't have any negative thoughts about who he could meet, who was following them or even what dangers Jack would be in. He was oblivious to the drama unfolding on the Hudson. Charlie was loving the adventure of being a secret agent. He wasn't even missing Mum and Dad. Mum always said that he needed to remember that whenever the family was not together that there would be a mini version of Mum and Dad sitting on each of his shoulders looking out for him. Mum and Dad felt strangely close despite being thousands of miles away.

Time for some food. He swooped around looking for somewhere to buy some food. He spied a bright yellow sign with Hamwich splashed across it. He landed and delved into his bag for some money as onlookers gaped at the 'jet boy' who had just descended from the heavens.

A ham sandwich, potato chips and a fizzy drink later (well, Mum and Dad weren't here, they would never know) and Jet Boy was off again.

Approaching the Hudson River and Pier Fifty-seven, Charlie decided to take a recce of the situation to ensure he wasn't being followed before he entered the pier building. He stopped at the top of the nearest skyscraper with its seriously large (and old-looking) fans whirring away, circulating the air around the building. He put on his sunglasses and said, "Activate binoculars." The sunglasses began to zoom in to the pier. Charlie could see a deserted, decrepit building with holes in the corrugated roof. There were birds nesting in the girders that jutted out from the roof holes.

"Hmm, not really five star, Jack," Charlie muttered to himself.

There were pathways around both sides of the building, with a large rusty sliding door on the right hand side – further zooming in identified a large padlock on the outside – more work required. A jetty stretched out from the back right of the pathway into the Hudson but no boats were to be seen within a mile. In fact, further viewing showed that the jetty was crumbling into the water as the end support posts had rotted and were falling away. Charlie could not see the back of the building so he used the thermal imaging option on his sunglasses to check that there were no people inside or at the back of the building. He was satisfied that this was a safe place, or as safe as it could be at the current time, but decided to wait and watch for a few more minutes.

He sensed a presence behind him that startled him from his pier gazing, he swiftly turned around to find,— no-one! He took a few steps towards where he thought he had sensed someone and a noise came from behind him again, exactly where he had just walked from. No-one there!

The building fans stopped. Silence, an eerie silence, apart from the distant honking of taxi horns below. A metallic knock came from inside one of the fans. Charlie stood firm, waiting and watching again but this time not focusing on the pier, but on the 'no-one' that he knew was there. Deep breath. Charlie slowly but quietly pulled a stun gun from his rucksack. When fired, the gun would attack the target's nervous system and freeze their physical movements for approximately five minutes; no permanent damage but enough to escape, or at least get a decent head-start.

The fans started again which was a comforting sound, compared to the alternative of silence. Quick thinking, Charlie used the thermal imaging sunglasses on the fans but the interference created by the motion of the fan and the flow of air just made everything appear black and blank. "Useless," Charlie muttered again.

A radio crackled and in unison, four figures all dressed in black jumped from different fan units and aimed Taser guns at Charlie. In that moment, Charlie felt an odd sense of relief. Taser guns; they weren't trying to kill him. This was an opportunity then. Charlie fired the stun gun at the first two figures and they instantly fell to the floor, motionless. But the other two were quick to take advantage. Charlie managed to point and aim at one of them as he approached; he fell forward and toppled into Charlie, knocking the stun gun clean out of his hand and over the edge of the skyscraper. The last figure, dressed in black, including a black balaclava covering his face, spoke in a foreign accent that made every W sound like a V. "Ve know who you are vorking for. Surrender now or I vill fire." Charlie weighed up his options; surrender, fight, jump off the side of the building and use the jet engine (he decided that the edge of the building was not close enough and he would get Tasered) or get Tasered. None of these options seemed favourable. He couldn't even reach in to his bag for any gadgets or weapons as the figure was too near and he would react too quickly.

"I saw you in Mexico," the figure continued to talk. "You know I can fire vith accuracy, that dart that knocked you out was fired from fifty metres avay, ten metres will not be a problem for me. Don't do anything stupid."

Good advice, thought Charlie. This was 'the shadow', the man who was lurking in the shadows in the pyramid.

"Speak to me, young man. Ve know vhere you are from and who you are vorking for." The figure didn't want to shut up to allow Charlie time to think.

Did he really know who he was or was this just an act? Charlie contemplated.

"Who are you?" Charlie shouted back.

"I'm your friend if you do as you are told, or your vorst enemy if not," the figure replied.

"What's your name?" Charlie began to gain more confidence.

"Just call me K," the shadow responded.

"Kate? That's a girl's name," Charlie misheard.

"K, the letter K," the shadow replied angrily.

"How do you spell that?" Charlie chuckled.

"No more vasting my time, you are coming vith me," K jerked forward to grab Charlie and Charlie instinctively moved away from him and towards the edge of the building. He peered backwards over his shoulder at the seventy-storey drop below with no plans to avoid it.

At the same time K yelped out loud and he was on the deck. A lady dressed in a strange orange floppy hat, blue mack and red trainers appeared from behind one of the fans and had thrown an object that looked a bit like a boomerang, but it had tangled K's legs and he had fallen flat on his face. The lady followed this up by throwing another similar weapon at K's arms, tying them up. He was not going very far, very soon at all.

"Go," the lady whispered to Charlie, pointing to the stairwell that led to the lift for the building.

Charlie had to pass the lady to get to the stairwell. He stopped next to her. There was something familiar about her but he couldn't see her well enough under the ridiculously over-sized orange floppy hat to work out why. He could just make out a glimpse of a pair of eyes, they were green and friendly.

"Thank you, whoever you are," Charlie smiled at the lady who patted him on his head in return. He briefly looked back at K on the floor struggling around to free himself. He smiled again and punched the air. "K for Kerchow!"

Chapter 12
Pier 57: Charlie's View

Twenty-fifth October 2016
Charlie had been hiding in Pier Fifty-seven for the last few hours and no sign of Jack. He was beginning to get concerned. He expected them both to arrive at the same time but as he had hit trouble, he thought Jack might beat him there, but no sign. He had even had to smash the padlock on the rusty, old sliding door on the side of the unit without Jack's help – nothing that a large sledgehammer couldn't handle, though!

He decided to go and have a recce to check no-one was ready to pounce on him in the building, making his way back to the sliding door. As he slowly but purposefully approached the sliding door, it began to slowly slide open. He expected to see Jack's friendly face appear. The Shadow had found him.

He shot off like lightning in the direction of where he had settled down for the last few hours, the only way out was through that door so he had to buy some time by hiding. The Shadow shouted, "I have all ze time in ze vorld, no rush, little man. I vill find you very soon!" and he let out a haunting, bellowing laugh.

Charlie bunkered down behind a stack of wooden crates; not much cover, but some cover would delay his inevitable capture. He could hear his own breathing. He needed to slow down and quieten down for his own sake. Where was Jack? Still no sign of him.

Chapter 13
Pier 57: Jack's View

Twenty-fifth October 2016
Propelling his kayak frantically over the Hudson with his home-made paddle power to get to dry land as quickly as possible, Jack was heading directly for the quickest route from the river. A bird landed on his kayak, which stopped him for a split-second. That moment was enough to make him stop and think. He realised that he was probably heading directly back into the hands of the men in black; they may already be waiting for him despite the chaos on the Hudson involving their own men. He had no idea how many of them there were but it was definitely more than their two-man team.

Change of plan. Jack decided that he should use his energy to head directly to Pier fifty-seven from the river and avoid the welcome party awaiting him on the banks immediately in front of him. It might take him longer but it would be safer. He looked at his watch. "Activate location check," he instructed. A 3D map glowed upwards out of the watch and he could see that he was heading for Pier Eighty-four, he would need to paddle twenty-seven more piers to ensure his new plan was successful. It would be tiring but worth it.

Two hours later, he reached the jetty for Pier fifty-seven. Well, what should have been a jetty, but was just a few rotten loose planks of wood. He left the kayak in the water in case he needed an escape route and then he hauled himself up from the water, about six feet upwards, using the rotten wood as an aid, shuffling over the top of the pier's wooden boardwalk on his tummy. Maybe this adventure would help him decide what he wanted to do for a job when he was older. Maybe not even a secret agent but a ninja, with the kind of agility he had shown.

He clambered to his feet quickly so he could take in his surroundings. This was definitely an unused pier; rickety, unkempt, rotting, silent and even a bit spooky. Jack had no intention of them staying here for long. It was moments like this that made him think of home. A funny feeling filled his stomach but it wasn't homesickness, it was the instinct that something was not right. Charlie should be here but he knew his brother too well, he couldn't stay this quiet unless something was wrong. Something or someone was not right.

Jack checked his watch to review Charlie's whereabouts before he took any further steps. Charlie was definitely in the building, so why was he not keeping an eye out for him as they had agreed? First one there would keep looking every five minutes. Jack had arrived at the foot of the pier about seven minutes ago.

Then, he could hear a faint voice from inside the building: a man's voice; a man's voice that he did not recognise; a man's voice that sounded unpleasant and threatening. He checked his watch again for Charlie's location and then noticed a second heat presence: the man, only twenty metres from Charlie's position. Quick thinking and action required.

The sliding door at the side of the building appeared to be the only way in, therefore it was also the only way out. Jack set up an electric trip wire over the door, which would not only trip the man up if he got away but would also treat him to an electric shock that would knock him out for at least ten minutes. Pleased with his handiwork, Jack moved swiftly through the sliding door, which had had its padlock knocked off – very recently, as it was still hanging from the door.

He could hear the foreign voice shouting, "Little man, little man." He assumed he was referring to Charlie and it gave away his position.

Jack whispered, "Activate gang." A hologram of a number of people looking menacing, with guns and other weapons, surrounded Jack. Every time he moved the gang moved with him, even making additional footstep noises as he walked. They looked real and they were his new army, even if they couldn't shoot their guns or use their weapons. In fact, they couldn't even walk without Jack taking the steps for them.

The man was not far from them, he could hear his every move. Just round one more corner and they would be face to face. The man still hadn't found Charlie but he was standing only feet away from him. Charlie must be hiding, he was good at that when they played hide and seek when they were younger. He had once successfully hidden from Jack for a whole hour in his own wooden toy box. Jack remembered that Charlie came out of the toy box with a Santa hat on his head and glitter stuck to his face.

Deep breath and go for it. No, no, count of three and then go for it. Oh, just go for it, Jack decided. He burst around the corner, shouting and screaming at the man with his hologram army in tow. The man was startled, he panicked, didn't know which way to turn, there was only one way out. Jack pulled out a 'boom' grenade; it wouldn't harm the man but it would give him the biggest fright of his life. He pulled the pin on the grenade and threw it towards him. 'BOOM'. The din was deafening. The man disappeared, ran off, clearly there was another way out. All they heard was a distant splash, they assumed he'd found a quick exit through the rotten floorboards.

Jack de-activated the hologram army and knew exactly where to find his bro. He reached around the wooden stack of crates and put his arm around his brother. It was good to be back together again, the two of them – the three of them. Jack, Charlie and the Package.

Chapter 14
Boarding

'Cargo Ship, Pier 8, 8.40 a.m. tomorrow. Beware of men in all-black uniforms'. Charlie read the note that had been given to Jack by the mysterious man. They had compared stories and they had worked out that the mysterious man and woman who had helped them must be connected; they had worn the strangest, over-sized outfits, which matched. No-one could wear such unusual clothes that were the same without conferring on their choices, it was too much of a coincidence.

It was seven a.m. and the boys had slept rough for the night in Washington Square. They were kept company through some of the night by the continuous stream of chess players that had sat comfortably under the shade of the trees at the permanent chess tables. They had played until well gone midnight and whilst it kept them awake, it was a welcome distraction from the dangers of the last few hours. Chess was a game of strategy and Jack couldn't help but contemplate how the chess game was much like their own adventure. They had control of their next steps but their own strategy could be scuppered by their own opponents' next move; the Shadow, the men in black and whoever else was out there looking for them or the package, or both!

"How are we going to get on the ship, Jack?" Charlie enquired.

Jack didn't respond immediately, thinking about the best approach. He thought about the chess games that he had watched and noticed that the winners were normally the players that made the unexpected moves that took the opponents by surprise.

"If you were the Shadow, Charlie, how would you expect us to try and enter the ship?" Jack asked inquisitively.

"Hmmm." Charlie scratched his head in an over-exaggerated pause for thought. "If I was the Shadow, firstly, I would learn to say my words properly," he chuckled, "and I would expect us to sneak on to the ship and probably hide in a crate or a box of some sort."

"Exactly. How about we go for the surprise move? We walk straight up to the front of the ship and ask the captain for a lift!" Jack asked as a question, but toned as if it wasn't an option but precisely what they were going to do.

Charlie wasn't convinced but agreed it was definitely a surprise move – risky but a surprise!

Chapter 15
Homeward Bound?

"Hello," Jack shouted up from Pier Eight to the ship's crew. "Let me do the talking," he whispered to Charlie. The men barely looked up from their jobs and ignored them.

"Hey there," Jack tried again, waving frantically at the same time. Still no reaction. "Just leave it to me, Charlie," he whispered again. He decided to try a different tactic. He got an air horn out of his rucksack and let rip with a loud blast from the horn, only for it to be drowned out by the ship's own ridiculously loud horn.

"Jack, Jack, up here." There was Charlie, in the cabin of the ship, pressing the ship's horn.

"What? What? How?" Jack stumbled his own questions to himself.

"Come on, Jack, we've got a ride!" Charlie encouraged Jack.

Despite being delighted, he almost felt annoyed at Charlie for getting the attention of the crew before him. "I thought I told you to leave the talking to me?" he demanded.

Charlie just grinned back as Jack made his way up the gangplank on to the ship's deck.

The crew were all smiles and seemed very friendly. Most importantly, there was no sign of the men in black.

Jack caught sign of the name of the ship, the *Atlantic*. Finally, they were on the way home, sailing across the Atlantic Ocean back to the safety of rainy old England. The thought brought a little smile to Jack's face but he still managed to shoot Charlie a look of discontent as he appeared with a very tall, dark and muscular man. Jack instantly noticed that he was covered in tattoos of all different kinds of boats; pirate ships, cargo ships and liners were the ones that he could make out that peeked out from under his white vest. He was clearly passionate about his job.

"Welcome, brother. I'm Capitán Marley, welcome to ma crew," Captain Marley held out his hand to shake Jack's hand.

"Welcome to your crew?" Jack shot Charlie another look.

"Yay, you li'l bruvva here just got you a free Atlantic trip in exchange for ya labour, my friend," Captain Marley replied in a very broad Caribbean accent.

Jack paused, thought about it.

"Well done, Bro!" he unexpectedly praised his brother.

A huge smile broke out over Charlie's face, he loved it when his brother gave him praise. It didn't happen very often but Jack was clearly proud of him.

"You going to England?" Jack asked the captain.

"Yay, my friend, everyone wanna go to England. The Queen, the rain, London Town, Jimmy Farvey, man!" The last part got a huge reaction from the boys, Farvey was even famous here, in the docks of New York City.

"What do you want from us in exchange?" Jack continued. He was really growing to like Captain Marley.

"You work hard, cleaning, washing up, helping cook. I will give you free food, water, a bed and a ride across the Atlantic, my friend," the captain clarified.

Jack nodded, Charlie nodded. Captain Marley bumped fists with them both.

Captain Marley showed them around the ship. It was a cargo ship full of crates and boxes; he was very secretive about their contents but that didn't worry either of the boys, they were just grateful for the lift. He introduced them to every member of the crew, all of whom had nicknames; Goldtooth, Jimma, Pobble, Babble, Bazza, Boozer and Bizzy were the names that they could remember. They were to sleep in hammocks in the communal area with all the crew, this was turning in to an adventurous way home. The risk of the men in black was forgotten about, they felt safe and they trusted Captain Marley, he was a good man.

"Rockwalls, Rockwalls, I see you are on your way across the Atlantic." It was James, back in radio contact. He was still tracking their progress, which was reassuring. "Good work, boys, do you still have the package?"

"Yes, sir!" Charlie replied as he patted the rucksacks as if James could see them.

"Great work, really great work, boys," James responded in that well-educated posh voice of his.

The boys had found a quiet corner of the ship to talk in hushed tones to James. They brought him up to speed with all of the goings-on in the last few hours and days. As usual there was no indication of any surprise in James's voice, only concern for their safety.

"Listen, boys, I can't blow your cover so I'm going out of contact with you again. I will be here if you need me in an emergency, just shout the agreed code word to get back in contact. Good luck. Over and out." As usual, James ended the conversation bluntly and logged off the call.

"Code word?" Jack looked at Charlie. Charlie shrugged. They had forgotten the code word. Anyway, it didn't matter, within a couple of days they would be back in the UK, nothing could go wrong now. It was getting late and dark. They had worked for Captain Marley for a few hours so they made their way to the hammocks for a well-earned night's sleep. The motion of the boat soon helped them into a deep slumber.

Chapter 16
The Arrival Home

"Weeeeeelcooome to beautiful Morocco, my beautiful crew!" Captain Marley opened the doors to the sleeping area, at the same time letting in a stinging, bright sunlight. The stifling heat from outside hit the room.

"Morocco!" the boys, wide-eyed, shouted out loud in unison.

"This cannot be happening to us," Jack muttered over and over to himself. "This is a nightmare," he continued to grumble.

"We're on holiday!" Charlie squealed as he jumped off the deck of the boat into the warm sea water of the dock below.

"Do you not see our predicament, Charlie?" Jack shouted angrily at him from the deck. "This is serious! We should be heading home now, not in North Africa. This is a nightmare!"

"Chill out," Charlie shouted back. "This is fun!"

"Yeah, chill out, maaan!" It was Captain Marley. "You will be home soon, bruvva. I've found a buyer for my goods here in Morocco; he pay good money, man. Just need to meet him here in five hours, then we be heading for the White Cliffs of Dover, Jackie Boy." He put an arm around Jack to show that he was in safe hands.

"So, five hours and we will be setting sail?" Jack wanted confirmation from the captain.

"No, man. Five hours my buyer be meeting me. One hour to unload the crates. In six hours on the dot we will be back on the ocean waves, you have my word, bruvva." He winked at Jack. Jack could only muster a nod.

The Rockwalls decided to take a walk around the port of Tangier, a market port that was full of hustle and bustle. They took in the noise of the market traders hollering over each other; the aroma of spicy lamb meat cooking; the colourful reds, yellows and blues of the material being sold seemingly by every trader on the market; swarms of passengers descending from ships and liners that were docked in the port, flagging down taxis to take them to their next destination; the narrow alleyways and maze-like streets of the walled city. (Charlie found out from the captain that this was called a medina.) The place was a hive of activity, topped off with blazing hot sun burning down on the market and the boys; they were right in the middle of it all.

A man with a curly moustache and even curlier hair, wearing a small red hat, tried to get them to buy a nice new rug, but Charlie joked that it was not luxurious enough for Captain Marley's ship. Another market trader was pushing them to buy leather goods and a lady in traditional Moroccan dress was trying to force feed them raw herbs and spices before demanding they pay for them. A polite but firm, "La, shukran," ("No, thanks") from them both soon saw the market traders back off.

Despite the desire to get home, they were loving the atmosphere and decided to stop and eat some bread and spices under the shade of one of the trader's brightly coloured canopies. Carrying rucksacks in forty-degree temperatures was taking its toll and whilst they trusted

Captain Marley, they didn't want to leave the package unguarded. As they took a break, Jack was people watching and reflecting on the events of the previous few days and Charlie – well, Charlie was being Charlie and having a doze, oblivious to the chaos around him in the market place.

After about five hours, Jack was still watching the world go by. He had been watching two men bartering over the price of an old bicycle. They were hugely animated, waving their hands around and getting louder and louder as they seem to be getting to a price that they could agree on. Man number one was the seller, man number two was the buyer and he had already walked away twice in disgust at the price that the seller had given to him. Now, they were hugging each other as if they were the best of friends, a deal had been struck. Man number two rode away very unsteadily on his new purchase but with such pride on his face, he could have been travelling home in a brand new Ferrari. As he followed the man as he left the market place, something out of place caught his eye, a glint of light flashed in his eye from a distance, he could see a man with binoculars spying on them – dressed all in black!

"Charlie, Charlie, wake up!" Jack shouted. Charlie woke up, startled. "We've got to go right now, the men in black are back, they've found us!" Jack continued. He pointed to the man in the distance, who immediately realised that his cover had been blown.

They whipped up their rucksacks but the man was positioned between them and their place of safety on Marley's ship. They had to head to away from the ship and try to find the long way round to get back. They were heading into the maze of streets and alleyways in the walled city.

Binoculars, as the boys were now referring to him, was now beginning to pick up pace but clearly not trying to draw any attention to himself. The fact he was the only person that was stupid enough to wear black in this heat meant he was failing from his very first strides into the market. The market traders provided a great wall of protection for the boys, they were trying to sell Binoculars all sorts of products as he made his way through them. He just barged straight through them, much to their annoyance and the boys could hear the angry shouts wherever he was, which helped them keep track of his position.

The boys felt fairly speedy after their five hours of rest and were hurrying through the winding streets. The walls stretched probably four metres in the air so there was no way they could see Binoculars or he could see them. They were hopelessly lost in the maze of grey stone walls, just relying on their sense of direction to work out where to go.

Despite their pace, Binoculars was gaining on them fast, they could hear the kerfuffle following him. At one point he turned the corner and he could see them along one of the few straight streets and then, disaster. The boys ran down a dead end, an alleyway with no way out. They couldn't climb up the walls and they could see Binoculars heading straight for them. This was it, they were cornered. They began to hold up their hands as a sign of surrender when a trapdoor opened right under their feet. They fell straight through it, landing comfortably on a pile of rugs. A man covered from head to toe in bright red material pointed excitedly to the way they needed to go. They couldn't see his face but they had no choice but to head that way. They were now in an underground maze of alleyways, exactly the same as the streets above but with candles for light rather than the scorching sunlight.

The man led the way as they ran through people's houses, through lines of washing and jumped over crates of drinks. They turned left and then right, then left again, then left, then right. They had no idea where they were going. They ran and ran, sweating in the heat but it was run or be captured. The man then suddenly came to a halt. He pointed his nose to the ceiling and grunted something in his Moroccan tone. The boys scanned the ceiling as the man jumped up and grabbed a rope ladder; he indicated for the boys to climb the ladder. Both boys peered upwards and could see another trapdoor. They turned around to ask a question of the man, but he was gone! He had disappeared back into the underground village.

The boys had no time to dwell on his departure, they climbed the ladder, Charlie first while Jack held the ladder still, then Jack followed up through the trapdoor. Their eyes had to adjust as they entered back into the natural light. Squinting through the brightness, they could see the ship, but it wasn't at the dock, it was out at sea. Jack looked at his watch, they were late. Captain Marley's words came back to haunt him; "Six hours on the dot we will be back on the ocean waves."

Jack put his head in his hands. Charlie wrapped his arm around him. "Don't worry, Jack, we'll get home."

"Home is on my boat," a foreign voice came from behind them. It was the Shadow with about ten other men, all dressed in black, accompanying him. "Now, I vill take you on my ship and you vill give me my treasure." The men grabbed the Rockwalls and dragged them roughly on to a nearby ship that looked like an old-fashioned galleon. They were thrown, without their rucksacks, into the darkness below deck. Home felt a million miles away.

Chapter 17
The Darkness

Two days in the darkness in a small room below deck with no food, no gadgets and only some dusty hessian sacks to sleep on. The boys had fumbled around aimlessly and unsuccessfully in the dark to try to find a way out but over the last forty-eight hours they had familiarised themselves with every inch of the room. It had wooden panels for walls, wooden panels for a floor and, when Charlie had climbed on Jack's shoulders, he could just make out the wooden panels for a ceiling. The trapdoor was locked from the outside. There was no trapdoor in the floor. No way out.

The only thing keeping the boys informed of their whereabouts was James's hourly commentary in to their earpieces, he was tracking their position using one of the MI60 drones, which had locked its radar on to the ship. He provided as much information as possible in to his thirty-second update; any longer and he risked their communication being intercepted by their captors.

They knew that they had gone west from Morocco, back into the Atlantic Ocean and then headed north. They were currently in the Labrador Sea heading towards Baffin Bay on the east of Canada, with Greenland on the other side of the sea. James and the MI60 team had managed to tap into the boat's secure radio communications and the translation suggested that their next destination was Nuuk, the capital city of Greenland. Nuuk was located in the south-west of the country and was home to over a quarter of Greenland's whole population. MI60 intelligence also suggested that it was the home to a number of independent trade gangs that used the route for illegal buying and selling of all sorts of products including stolen valuables such as the treasure box. Their capture now made sense.

Neither Jack nor Charlie were particularly fond of the dark but they found that spending so long in this state meant it almost became normal; conquering your fears often meant facing them directly.

A series of bolts and locks were noisily shifting on the wooden panels on the ceiling, they were being unlocked. This was followed by a blast of blinding sunlight coming from the roof above; finally they were about to come out of the room. "Agua," a man shouted down to them, threw something down into the room which made them both jump and slammed the door shut. Maybe not!

The thirst-quenching water was more than welcome which made them feel strangely grateful to the crew, as if they were hotel staff waiting on them. Hours of seclusion did odd things to your mind and small things all of a sudden become the major things. A glass of water was now a luxury. Hours before, it was freely accessible and not even thought about.

"Rockwalls come in, Rockwalls come in." It was James.

"Hi, James," Charlie responded as if it was an everyday conversation.

"Charlie, please use the communication etiquette," James retorted.

"Rockwalls checking in, sorry, James." Charlie pulled a face at Jack then realised he couldn't see him in the dark. "Someone's got out of the wrong side of the bed," he whispered to Jack.

"I heard that, Charlie," James snapped.

"Please use the communication etiquette, James, thank you," Charlie said cheekily.

"Stop wasting our time, Rockwalls," James continued with his snappy attitude and before there was any further delay he continued with more information. "You will be in Nuuk in approximately twenty-four hours. There will be a welcome party for you there, the world-renowned Comercio Gang, around one hundred of the most feared trade gangsters. If you reach Nuuk, it is likely that you won't get out. I won't say any more than that. That means you have twenty-four hours to get out of the space that you are in and rescue yourselves. You are too far trapped for our team to get in to you, but if you can get yourselves on to the deck, then we can get a helicopter to you. Running out of time, speak in sixty minutes. Over and out." He was gone again.

The boys were alone with the need to develop an escape plan with no rucksacks, no gadgets, no help. It almost felt like no hope.

After ten minutes of contemplation, Charlie shot up from his pile of hessian sacks. "I've got it! Think about what we are good at – or more importantly, what Mum and Dad say we are good at."

Jack replied, "Football? Cricket? Spellings? Emptying the dishwasher? How are any of those skills going to help?"

"No, no," Charlie shook his head. "When Mum or Dad are in a bad mood, what do they say we are the best at?"

"Annoying them!" Jack shouted a little too loudly. "But I still don't get it."

Charlie took a deep breath as he thought carefully about his explanation.

"Well, we can only get out if they open the door, we can't open it from this side. Therefore, we need to get them to open the door." He put heavy emphasis on the word 'them'. "How do we get them to open the door? Be annoying. We make as much noise as we can. We shout, we bang on the wooden floors, walls and ceiling. We keep going and going. We annoy them enough for them to try to come and shut us up and then, bang, we hit them and exit."

"It could work," Jack replied cautiously. "I've just felt a loose floorboard, if we can snap it off or lever it upwards then we could use it as a weapon. Remember the advice that James gave us in training, use your surroundings to your advantage, observe your environment and then use the environment better than your enemy. We have three things in our environment; sacks – which are useless – wood and us!"

"Let's use the wood and us then." Charlie went for a high five with Jack but then again realised he couldn't see him.

"Let's wait until night-time when they are trying to sleep, everything sounds louder and scarier at night. We will ask James to let us know when the crew are likely to be asleep," Jack suggested.

"Let's do it! And don't write off using those sacks yet, I have a plan," Charlie said.

You couldn't see it in the pitch black but the Rockwalls had a glint in their eye. They knew they would soon be back on the front foot.

Chapter 18
The Escape

Seven hours later, seven more points of radio contact with James and seven hours making a ten foot long rope from the hessian sacks. Who said they were useless!

James gave the confirmation that the majority of the crew were now fast asleep in their bunks. Only three crew members were patrolling the decks and it would take the rest of the crew about seventy-five seconds to respond to any disturbance; sufficient time for their plan to take effect.

Charlie climbed back on to Jack's shoulders to hang the rope of sacks from the protruding hinge of the trapdoor. He then tested it by hanging from it with all his weight; it was solid.

Jack used all of his strength to pull up the loose floorboard, as quietly as possible, hoping not to create the loud disturbance too early. He then spent half an hour practising using the plank of wood as a weapon. It was too bulky to use like a light sabre and too blunt to use as a sword, so he just needed to be able to use the sheer weight of the wood to be able to temporarily knock the person out; this required power rather than skill. He would give it a go but he only had one chance.

James came back on to the radio to confirm the go ahead, outline the three crew members' positions on the boat and help draw a virtual map in their minds of the layout of the ship when they reached the decks. With only seventy-five seconds, they had no time to familiarise themselves with their surroundings when they reached the deck, they needed to get straight on with the plan of action. James disappeared from the comms with his usual abruptness.

"Here it goes then, buddy, are you ready?" Jack said to Charlie.

"Let me just get comfortable," Charlie said as he fidgeted around at the top of the rope to ensure he could spend at least five minutes in the position. "Okay, thumbs up," Charlie confirmed.

"One, two, three, let's go for it!" Jack shouted. Charlie rattled the trapdoor and banged his fist on the ceiling of the room. Jack started whacking the plank of wood on all surfaces around him; the walls and the floor. They both started yelling at the tops of their voices, shrieking, screaming, hollering, anything that would make a distinct noise. No sooner had they started and a stark voice came through the crack around the edge of the trapdoor.

"You boys cut that out!" the voice shouted angrily in, surprisingly, an American accent.

"No," Jack shouted obstinately.

"If you wake up the rest of the crew, you will be in for it and I will be in trouble as well. It's best for all of us if you shut up right now!" and then the line that said that the plan was on track. "Don't let me come down there and make you stop!"

"No," Jack repeated loudly as the din just continued.

"Right, I warned you!" the voice shouted aggressively.

The bolts began to unlock. Charlie stopped making the noise while Jack carried on. Charlie braced himself for the next move. The locks were being unlocked with pace and anger, probably making as much noise as Jack was. Then the movement slowed down as the creaking of the hinges began. Charlie held his breath.

The outline of the Voice's figure could now be seen through the hole in the trapdoor but Charlie had to wait for his moment. Go too early and the plan would fail, it was a test of nerve. The Voice slowly poked his head through the trapdoor; he was trying to let his night vision settle as he peered into the darkness in the same way that Jack and Charlie's vision had to adjust to the moonlight shining through.

The moment came. Charlie jumped and wrapped his whole body around the Voice's neck, toppling him through the trapdoor and to the ground, with Charlie twisting in flight to ensure he landed on top of him. He hit the ground with an almighty thud. By this time, Jack had ceased making the noise and was preparing himself to enter into 'gladiator' mode with his plank of wood. But there was no movement from the Voice. Charlie was up and on his feet but the Voice remained still; he was out cold. Jack checked his breathing; he was still breathing. He dropped the wood.

"Right, go, go, go, we've lost ten seconds already," Jack instructed.

They both shimmied up the rope to the trapdoor and swung themselves up through the trapdoor like the monkeys at their local zoo. Effortless!

Using the description given by James, they could see Plan A of trying to recover their rucksacks was blocked off by the other two crew members who were on guard. They were heading straight towards them but had not quite made out the situation in front of them. Plan B, the 'just get the hell out of there' plan kicked in. The boys headed straight for the lifeboats on the outside of the ship and dived into one. Jack released the ropes holding the lifeboat to the ship and they dropped about twenty feet into the water with a huge splash. If the crew were still asleep, then they most definitely wouldn't be now. The lifeboat was free and Charlie started rowing whilst Jack kept lookout at the ship. The two crew members were taking aim with their guns and bullets pinged all around them, but they were rowing in the opposite direction to the ship. The ship would have a wide turning circle so it would take them time to catch them up, they just hoped James could deliver on his side of the plan.

More bullets. Jack could make out a further seven men on the ship's deck, firing away. One bullet punctured the lifeboat then another and another, they were going down, they were sinking almost immediately. The plan was in danger of failing.

"Lifejacket, Jack, put it on quickly." Charlie had already placed his around his head and had pulled the self-inflator toggle. Jack hurriedly put on his lifejacket as bullets whizzed by their heads with more and more damage to the lifeboats. It was dark but the crew knew which direction they were heading. Torchlight kept on scanning over the sea and sky, but never quite identified their exact location.

"We'll be safer in the water now, Jack, they have guessed our location and bullets are hitting every few seconds. Dive in. One, two, three, go!" Charlie called out.

They both dived into the ice-cold sea water and swam to put distance between them and the lifeboat. Any more than two minutes in sub-zero water temperatures would be life threatening. "Come on, James," shouted Jack. At that exact point, the sound of a chopper circling overhead came into earshot with a spotlight searching the water. "That was impressive," Jack shouted as if he had conjured up the helicopter by shouting for James to hurry up.

Without any indication that they had been found, a winch was sent down to them with a man on the end of it. "Get on here," he shouted. Both boys swam towards him and their feet were lifted away from the icy water. Saved again, home was now in sight, again!

Chapter 19
The Hard Side of the Job

The boys were being checked out by the on-board doctor and were wrapped in foil blankets to get their core body temperatures back up to safe levels. The doctor gave them the all clear. Then that familiar voice of James came in over the noise of the helicopter. This time it was not a radio voice; he was present in the chopper. His face had never been so welcoming to the boys but that soon changed, he had a very serious and unemotional look on his face.

"MI60 do not fail their operations, boys. We do not have the package and we have our essential equipment, your backpacks, in the hands of serious criminals. This mission is not over for you yet." James was very straight talking but this time he was particularly assertive with his instructions.

"But we've only just managed to escape," Jack immediately responded, half pleading and half annoyed.

"No, we managed to escape. We are one team and we will be going back to complete the mission as one team. I know you think I am being hard on you and you are only boys, but you are our best hope and quite honestly, you are the best agents we have had since, since—" James paused as if he had stopped himself saying something that he shouldn't. "Since two of our agents retired from the business over seven years ago."

"Who were they?" Charlie chirped up, very proud of his comments.

"That's not important and their identities will be kept secret, much as yours will be as well," James replied, now slightly calmer.

"Okay," Jack interrupted. "We don't want to fail, we can't fail. Crosses don't fail!"

"Please keep with the department's code of secrecy, Jack. Rockwalls, not your surname," James corrected him.

"Rockwalls, then!" Jack responded, slightly annoyed at James's sharpness with him even though he knew he was right. The pilot, the doctor and other air crew members didn't actually know Jack and Charlie's real identity.

"What next?" Charlie asked.

"We will take you to Nuuk and you will recover the package from the heart of the gang's headquarters. We will give you new gadgets until you can retrieve your rucksacks, but they will be limited and you will be at full power once the backpacks are recovered. You choose which order you wish to undertake the tasks, but my recommendation would be backpacks first, package second. Arm yourself to the max. This gang is one of the most dangerous that any of our agents have faced." James paused for thought at that comment. This was the first show of emotion from him and gave the boys an inkling of the risks that they would face.

Unfazed by the dangerous proposition, Jack slapped a reassuring hand on James's back.

Charlie's enthusiasm took over. "Right, we need some new gadgets to play with!"

The Rockwalls were back on with the mission.

Chapter 20
Nuuk, Greenland: Gang HQ

Cold suits on. Snow goggles on. Mission back on.

Charlie had always envisioned Greenland as a bright, white and magical place where dreams come true. The helicopter had been unable to land due to a snow storm and had winched them down into a total whiteout. They couldn't see four inches beyond their nose. If they stayed still, they would freeze and if they moved, they were at risk of getting lost or even stepping into a crevasse or other dangers. They decided the risk of moving was lower and got on their feet.

They had been dropped about five kilometres from Nuuk and they needed to approach from this point with caution. Jack thought to himself how grey and depressing the place looked even as the snowstorm began to die down. There was low cloud, it was minus twenty degrees and the icy edge just made him feel like no-one could make this feel homely. The thought that they were about to confront one of the deadliest gangs just added to his views of the place.

Before they reached the point of contact they had just the small obstacle of Sermitsiaq – one thousand two hundred and ten metres of ice-covered mountain. They could go round it but it would take four days. Going over it should only take them twelve hours – no decision to be made.

The Rockwalls reached the base of the mountain and decided to take in some of the super-charged food that they'd become accustomed to eating. They then put on their crampons, took out their ice axes and commenced climbing, just like James had shown them four hours earlier when the chopper stopped to refuel in East Canada. No time wasted.

Seven hours later they had reached the summit, slightly behind schedule. The view was absolutely stunning, sheer whiteness as far as the eye could see with the odd leafless tree poking out from the blanket of snow. Nuuk was a city so different to any other city they had seen. Most of the buildings were no more than two storeys high, with only two significant landmarks. Nuuk Cathedral, as their watches informed them, was a prominent wooden red structure, with the only clue that it was a religious building being the square steeple at its peak. The other landmark was far more fitting of a city building: the Højhus Jagtvej Nord, the tallest building in the whole of Greenland at thirty-eight metres and thirteen floors high.

As much as they would have liked to sit and stare at the beauty of the place, they had a mission to complete. Their initial thoughts of Greenland were changing, the greyness had disappeared.

"We're behind, Jack, we need to catch up some time. Any ideas?" Charlie questioned.

"Already been thinking about this one. Ever fancied trying snowboarding?" Jack answered with a question.

"We don't have our rucksacks, Jack, we can't conjure up a snowboard from thin air."

"Our rucksacks aren't everything, Charlie. Look around you, be resourceful," Jack insisted.

"I see snow, snow and more snow," Charlie observed.

"The first of two ingredients for snowboarding," Jack announced. "What else do you see? Look closely."

Charlie spun around on his heels. Sometimes he wished Jack would just get on with it and tell him what he was thinking rather than play games. Then, bingo, he saw it, the only evidence that any other human life had reached this summit; a wooden sign that probably announced the summit point in Eskimo-Aleut, the local language.

They heaved the sign down with their bare hands, which sounds harder work than it actually was. The reality was that the sign was already leaning and ready to fall over, so they just needed to give it a helping hand. Conveniently, the sign was made of two side faces of plywood on a wooden frame. They used their limited tools to lever the two faces off the frame and there they had their new snowboards, ready to go.

Jack went first to lead the way and set the route. It took a couple of false starts, with a landing in the wet snow as a reward but they were soon cutting a swathe down the mountain and, within two hours, they were down. Schedule blown away, now to go into battle!

The GPS co-ordinates of the gang headquarters were programmed into the boys' watches. They were only eight hundred metres away so they had to proceed cautiously. Eight hundred metres, seven hundred, six hundred, five hundred, four hundred. No sign of anyone at all, never mind the gang. Three hundred, two hundred, one hundred metres. Still no-one. Fifty metres, ten metres, and then they arrived on the doorstep of a nondescript blue wooden two-storey building. It didn't look much like the home of a dangerous gang but they had come to trust the technology and they knew to expect the unexpected.

Charlie thrust himself forward to knock on the door. Jack grabbed him just in time. "What are you doing?" he whispered through gritted teeth.

"Seeing if anyone is in?" Charlie said innocently.

"And then what will you do when one of the gang answers the door?" Jack said, clearly annoyed.

"Ask for my rucksack back?" Charlie began chuckling and Jack couldn't help but see the funny side. They had a moment of stifled laughter before they gathered themselves together again.

"Right, let's try around the back," Charlie suggested.

They crept around the side of the building, with the only clue that there was a crowd of people using the property being the amount of rubbish that they had to step around, through or over. The gang clearly liked ready meals; bags and bags of empty containers littered the path. Jack tripped over one of the bags and saved his fall by landing on all fours.

"Nice find," Charlie dipped down to the bag that Jack had fallen over. As he straightened up, he was dangling both of their rucksacks from each of his index fingers and swinging them in the air.

"I don't believe it, they had the most high technology bags in the world and they throw them away like rubbish. They might be deadly but they're certainly not clever," Jack muttered as he got back to his feet.

They both clambered to get their rucksacks back on. The bags had become their comfort blankets. Jack had likened his rucksack to Superman's cape; it changed his powers from an everyday boy to a superhero secret agent. However, it couldn't put the package back into their possession, that was something that they had to do on their own.

Even though the rucksacks provided further protection from the freezing temperatures, the boys had slowed their pace down since their snowboarding expedition and they were now starting to feel the cold. They needed to either get inside or up the pace a little. They decided that inside was their preferred option and they had found an unlocked door just beyond the strewn rubbish on the side of the building. They had no idea what to expect beyond the door but they pulled out their Tasers from the rucksacks as a precaution.

The door was an old wooden door with the white paint flaking off and as they slowly edged it open, it let out an almighty creak, at which point they had to just go for it, as whoever was behind it now knew someone was entering the building. They rushed forward together into what could have been any home's family kitchen with green painted cupboards, pale coloured worktops, a kettle, toaster and even a calendar on the wall (which hadn't been turned over for a few months, it was still on May). No sign of life, no sign of movement, so they proceeded through the only internal door and moved into a hallway that had one more door leading off it and stairs leading to the first floor.

Charlie prodded the door open and then shot behind the wall, expecting someone to shoot at them or come charging through to tackle them. Again, no movement so they moved into the room with purpose and their Tasers pointing in front of them. The room was empty, with a window looking out at the front aspect of the building and there in the middle of the room was a large safe.

Jack inspected the safe closely. "It's in there, I know it's in there, the package is in there." The safe was a digital coded safe but they couldn't understand why the gang had left it unguarded. Maybe they weren't used to people having the courage to stroll straight into their gang headquarters.

"How do you fancy a bit of safe-cracking, Charlie?" Jack questioned his brother playfully.

"Well, I've tried flying without a plane, sailing on a ship, trekking though jungles, climbing a mountain, snowboarding—I'm sure our skills can stretch to putting a few numbers into a safe!" Charlie replied.

"And here is the tool that will do the trick," Jack pointed to his watch.

He reached down to the safe and scanned it with the laser on his watch. He instructed, "Safe code cracker," into the watch. There was a short delay and then a six-digit number appeared on his watch. All he had to do was type it into the safe lock and it would pop open to reveal its contents.

"Jack, there are four, no, five, no, eight men approaching. They are all dressed in black. One of them is K, you know, the Shadow," Charlie shouted, startled by the sudden dilemma.

Jack didn't reply and quickly typed in the safe number; it opened with a ping. There in front of them was not just the package but loads of other expensive-looking treasures. But they didn't have time to inspect the other things. He grabbed the treasure box, which was as still as golden and sparkly as ever, and shoved it into his rucksack.

"The window opens, Jack, come on, we're going out here." Charlie pointed through the blinds that were over the front window and was already making his way through it. They could hear the men making their way to the side door, the rustle of rubbish bags giving them away.

Then the first man began to open the door at the same time as Jack was following Charlie out of the window. His bag snagged on the corner of the window and it slammed shut with a thud.

No sooner had that happened than a face came into view the other side of the glass, glaring at them, puzzled as to who could possibly infiltrate their HQ. The shock was written over all three faces; the gang member's, Jack's and Charlie's. The face started shouting to his fellow gang members with extreme urgency. Jack shouted, "Run, just run," as he pointed down the road towards the town.

They had probably travelled about one hundred metres before the first sign of them being chased was evident. It wasn't footsteps, it wasn't shouting; it was the now familiar sound of bullets shooting past them. The roads had been cleared of snow in this part of the town so the grip on the road was fine but in their extra warm clothing, it was particularly difficult, overheating and restricted movement causing problems. They reached a corner without any of the shots hitting their target, namely the Rockwalls. In the distance, Charlie spotted some water, maybe a lake. "Let's head there, we're not going to shake them off by running but there may be some crowds of people where we can lose them," he panted through deep breaths.

No further communication needed, they veered towards the lake; the gang were catching them up. The men in black were not firing as regularly now, but more focused on closing the gap.

As the lake came further into view, it became apparent that there were no crowds, in fact no-one around at all. All that was on show was a jetty with a seaplane moored. Decision time, what should they do now?

"Ever flown a plane, Jack?" Charlie pointing the way again.

"Nope, but it's our only option," Jack replied. "You go in first and I will detach the mooring ropes. Use your watch to activate the autopilot mode, it might work, who knows!"

The gang were now only fifty metres behind them, catching them up with every stride but still only the odd gunshot flashing by the boys. They expected to be on the end of a barrage of bullets but it had not arrived.

They reached the seaplane, just hoping that there was no-one in it and that it was not locked. This seemed like the kind of town where everyone left everything unlocked and they were in luck; it was empty and the door was open. Charlie dived in and started the watch scanning and instructed, "Activate seaplane autopilot."

Jack dived in almost straight after him. "You need to instruct a destination else the plane won't go anywhere!"

"Oh, erm, erm, activate seaplane autopilot to England," Charlie eventually clarified the instruction.

The plane immediately started up but Jack had not had time to release the mooring rope. The gang were now right on them as the plane started but it was struggling to pull away with the rope holding it in place. One of the gang was pulling at the door but Jack had had the foresight to lock it; then, bang, the gunshots started, one of them directly aimed at the door in an attempt to blow the lock open.

The seaplane began to win its battle with the rope and it made its way along the side of the jetty with the gang now struggling to keep up. The rope was now taut and instead of holding the plane back, it ripped up the jetty, throwing the gang members into the water, the shots dying down at the same time. One of the gang members was more determined and had thrown himself on the landing skis of the seaplane. He was clinging on, shouting angrily at the boys. It was K, their nemesis.

K was swinging by one hand as the seaplane gathered height. They were still over the lake but ascending very sharply in the air. He was trying to use the momentum of the plane's movement to swing his legs up and on to the skis so he could enter through the damaged door on Jack's side of the plane. He was like a pendulum in an old grandfather clock, swinging away in rhythm as the plane began to bank around. Then as the plane changed direction, it gave him the leverage to get his feet wrapped around one of the skis and he hauled himself up on all fours. All the time the boys were watching the goings-on, awaiting the inevitable fall from height into the lake below, but K was resilient and determined and was not to be defeated. That was until Jack waited until K had crawled all the way along the ski to the door and he whacked the door open and knocked K off balance. He toppled over, first on to his side, then on to his back and then, as if in slow motion, he disappeared off the edge, his arms flailing like a windmill, desperately trying to grab hold of anything to stop him falling but it was too late. The boys watched as he plummeted all the way back into the lake from about seventy-five metres in altitude. Through their binoculars they watched him dip under the water for a few seconds, then re-emerge, waving his arms about for help. K was alive but he wasn't going to stop the Rockwalls returning home with the package.

Jack and Charlie high fived, relieved that their close call was just that and nothing more than that. Jack gave it the 'boof, boof, boof' salute. This was mission complete. This was the plane home.

"Good work, boys. I see you are heading for home, stay vigilant, stay alert and we will see you in a few hours," the comforting voice of James filled the cockpit of the plane.

Chapter 21
Not Again!

Waaaaaarp! Waaaaaarp! Waaaaaaarp! Waaaaaaaarp!

The boys awoke immediately from their slumber with a shock. The whole of the cockpit was alive with alarms, warning lights and buzzers going off!

'Low Fuel' was flashing on the dashboard – how could that be? The boys had only checked the fuel an hour before, following James's advice and it had been assessed as having well over twenty-four hours of flying time.

Charlie scanned his watch over the entire cockpit and instructed, "Diagnostic test on low fuel detection." The watch performed an immediate test and returned the answer on the face of the watch:

BULLET HOLE IN FUEL TANK

"Oh, man!" Charlie let out a big sigh. "Here we go again!"

He showed the watch to Jack, who threw his hands up in the air in a dramatic show of frustration. "We're going down!" Jack declared.

"Maybe, but what if we try to do a controlled crash landing?" Charlie enquired.

"Hmmm, the choices are, we eject from the plane, but that means the plane could land anywhere and put others in danger. We crash land or we just crash," Jack laid out the options.

"We are just over Iceland so I say, let's go for the crash landing," Charlie said, quite assertively.

"Agreed, let's do it," Jack responded.

The boys strapped themselves into the pilot and co-pilot seats, alarms still blaring away. Jack provided the instruction, "Activate autopilot crash land in Iceland." There was no delay in the response; the seaplane immediately pointed its nose down and began heading towards the ground.

Jack and Charlie had no idea what to expect. They were in the emergency landing position that they had seen so many times demonstrated by the air stewardesses on the aeroplanes to their family holidays. It was only a matter of seconds before the plane reached ground level. The Rockwalls braced themselves.

There was an immediate crunching noise from underneath the plane; it was the landing skis snapping off, which pushed the plane in to a full three hundred and sixty degree spin. They had landed on icy ground and the plane continued rotating on its underbelly for well over two hundred metres before it smashed into a clump of trees, slowing down the pace and the spin. The tail of the plane had ripped off and was left behind, tangled in the trees. A vacuum of wind came flushing through the plane, straight into the cockpit, cleanly pushing out the front window. The plane came to rest right on the edge of a lake, in fact, RIGHT on the edge of a lake. So close, the front of the plane was angled into the water with the destroyed back end of the plane pointing towards the sky. The boys were at high risk of sinking to the bottom of the lake with the remains of the plane.

Battered, bruised and with a few cuts, but otherwise they were in relatively good condition considering the trauma that they had just been through. The boys responded immediately, both of them noticing the immediate danger that presented to them. They whipped up their rucksacks and raced to the rear of the plane, the ice underneath cracking loudly with the weight and instability of the carcass of the plane. The plane started to slip down further into the water, making it steeper and harder for the boys to reach the back. They were going under but with one last massive effort Jack managed to reach the metallic burred opening that was now the furthest point of the plane, he clung on with the tips of his fingers and slowly pulled himself up and over the edge with Charlie not far behind him. As he fell out of the back of the plane, he grabbed Charlie's hand and they clattered to the ground in a heap. At that very moment, the whole plane disappeared, nose to tail, deep into the lake. Another narrow escape!

The boys lay there for ten minutes without moving, just puffing and panting as they lay awkwardly on top of their rucksacks, getting their breath back after the exertion and trying to make sense of yet another failed effort to get home. Charlie was the first to move and he wrapped his hand around Jack's and pulled him up off the sodden, icy ground. No words were spoken.

They trekked along with just white landscape for company, until after about half an hour they came across a little wooden hut. It looked deserted and their instincts were right. It was just a wooden hut, nothing in it at all apart from two wet, cold and shivering secret agents. A bitter icy wind had begun to surface outside so they decided that their best chance of survival was to take cover until it died down.

Jack tried contacting James about their predicament but the radio communications were down. Maybe the crash had caused some damage to their kit or even the weather was creating a barrier to the secure connection. Whatever the reason, they were relying on their own resilience to succeed. Resting up for a bit was the right decision.

Chapter 22
More Company

A shuffle of feet was heard outside the door of the hut. Jack and Charlie both shot up from their comfortable positions on the floor. The door bolted open, a gloved hand launched something into the room and slammed the door shut again.

The attention went from the door to the thing that had been thrown into the hut, hesitation by the boys deciding whether to head for the person or the object. As if it was all second nature, they split the tasks without speaking. Jack went for the object, Charlie directed himself towards the door.

The door was locked. The object was a canister that was now leaking gas. The Rockwalls were being gassed. Somehow the gang had followed and hunted them down.

"This cannot be happening," Jack blurted out. There was no way out of this one.

As the gas took effect, Jack and Charlie collapsed on the floor, they were back in the hands of the Comercio Gang—the men in black!

Chapter 23
Really?

The boys started arousing at the same time, probably helped by their new hosts throwing a bucket of water over their faces to bring them around. They were both suffering from the effects of the gas; blurry eyes, pounding heads and impaired hearing.

There were muffled voices and both of the boys were lying down, on what felt like airbeds on the floor, detecting a couple of people moving around them.

After twenty minutes of drifting in and out of consciousness, Jack and Charlie started coming around, eyesight beginning to focus and sensitivity of hearing coming back to normal. Now the senses were coming back into play, Jack felt a horrible feeling of dread wash over him. They were captive once again. The men in black had got the upper hand.

"Welcome back, Rockwalls!" It was James. The radio communications must have been fixed, but listen to the words. 'Welcome back'?

The boys jumped up from their makeshift beds at exactly the same time. The voice wasn't over the radio, it was in the room.

"Sorry we had to gas you, boys, but we had to make sure that there was no-one else with you in that hut. We didn't want to be compromised by the Comercio Gang. You have had a good sleep, twenty-four hours' kip is pretty impressive, you must be tired!" James updated them.

Jack and Charlie couldn't quite take it all in. They did not respond. They scoped the room, then it hit them. They were back at the toy shop, the starting point of the adventure!

"We're home! Yes, we're home," Charlie shouted, arms in the air as if he had won the World Cup.

"We're home, we're home," Jack followed on with the hysteria.

"You've done a great job, Rockwalls, mission complete," James stated and he held up the treasure box, the package.

Jack shook James's hand in a mature, grown-up way. Charlie just flung his arms around James with a big hug, James looking slightly awkward with this response. There could not have been a prouder look on the boys' faces if they had actually won the World Cup. They had just completed a mission for MI60, the most secret of all national services—and loved it!

"You boys have served your country exceptionally well and we have a special message for you from a very important person, but you must not share this with anyone. We trust you," James built up the tension. The boys just nodded, still shocked.

"Look at your watches," James instructed.

Jack and Charlie did as they were told and gazed at their watches.

Right in front of them on the face of the watch appeared a clear image of the Queen. Yes, the Queen of England. The message began, with both boys open-mouthed.

"To my secret agents, thank you for serving your country in such an honourable, brave and selfless way. I have been told of the courage that you have shown in rescuing one of the most precious artefacts that this country has ever seen. The box that you have retrieved has been part of the royal heirloom for over four hundred years. Wars have been fought over its ownership and it is the most valuable and sentimental treasure in the world. I thank you for its safe return and you will be forever part of this great country's history. You are at the start of your career in our secret service and I wish you well for your future. Thank you and good luck." The Queen's image then disappeared.

Charlie looked at Jack, Jack looked at Charlie, total disbelief over their faces.

"You have made Her Majesty proud, boys. We can't give you medals, as that would endanger your cover and the secrecy of the service. You will, however, go down in the records as holding the Medal of Bravery. One day, someone will find out about MI60 and these records will become public knowledge. It may be five years, ten years or a hundred years' time but your heroics will be there for all to see.

"Now, your mum and dad will be here in twenty minutes. Go get freshened up, change your clothes and remember, you have been to Disney World." James paused for breath and watched the lads disappear into the next room to get changed without any further conversation. The boys were reeling from the pace at which the story was unfolding.

"And leave those rucksacks and watches here, you can't take them with you," James followed up.

Charlie gave a huffy response, he was hoping to take his packed lunch to school in that rucksack. Imagine the attention he would get!

Twenty minutes later, Mum and Dad arrived, oblivious to the journey that they had been on. Jack and Charlie just wrapped themselves in a big family hug, they were exhausted but exhilarated to be home.

"How was the adventure, monkey boys?" Mum asked.

"It was the most amazing adventure ever," Jack honestly declared.

"You look really tired, are you sure you didn't disappear on a world trip?" Dad joked.

If only they knew!

Chapter 24
Boxing Day 2017

The adventure was over and Jack and Charlie had returned to being mischievous, boisterous schoolboys; they had returned to being the Cross brothers. The mission now seemed like a dream, the best ever dream, but this dream had happened while they were wide awake. They were now back to the normal routine.

It was freezing cold outside, but not as cold as they had experienced in Greenland or Iceland. They were just getting ready to go out for the annual family Boxing Day meal. Mum and Dad were busy getting their shoes on in the hallway; the boys were doing their usual messing around rather than getting ready.

"Will one of you boys go upstairs and get my scarf, please?" Mum requested.

"Race you!" Charlie pushed Jack away and started running up the stairs with Jack taking up the challenge and in hot pursuit.

They rummaged around in all of Mum and Dad's drawers but couldn't find the scarf.

"Muuuuum, where is it?" Charlie yawped.

"It's in the storage box on the landing," Mum replied.

Jack got there first, opened up the box and began sorting through the layers and layers of warm clothes, gloves, scarves and hats.

Then, he stopped.

Charlie came next to him. "What's up?"

Jack pointed his head towards the box.

Charlie peered in.

There in front of them were two orange floppy hats and two blue macks.

Charlie thought back to New York, the woman on the roof who had saved him. Jack had already cast his mind back to the man near the pier, who had dropped the newspaper in his lap.

The cogs turned, they sprung a look of surprise.

"Mum and Dad are MI60 agents!"